Also by Mylisa Larsen
Playing Through the Turnaround

QUAGMIRE T
COULDN'T B

QUAGMIRE TIARELLO COULDN'T BE BETTER

MYLISA LARSEN

CLARION BOOKS
An Imprint of HarperCollins*Publishers*

Clarion Books is an imprint of HarperCollins Publishers.

Quagmire Tiarello Couldn't Be Better
Copyright © 2024 by Mylisa Larsen
All rights reserved. Printed in the United States of America.
No part of this book may be used or reproduced in any manner whatsoever
without written permission except in the case of brief quotations embodied
in critical articles and reviews. For information, address HarperCollins
Children's Books, a division of HarperCollins Publishers,
195 Broadway, New York, NY 10007.
www.harpercollinschildrens.com

Library of Congress Control Number: 2023949830
ISBN 978-0-06-332466-4

Typography by Chris Kwon
24 25 26 27 28 LBC 5 4 3 2 1
First Edition

For all the kids I've met through the years who have been holding up a whole lot of their worlds. You have taught me a lot about empathy and compassion and resilience.

And you're what made me want to write this book.

Thank you. I see you.

ONE

When Principal Deming asked Quagmire Tiarello what he was planning on doing with the first day of his summer vacation, Quag did not tell him that he planned on sleeping in until at least noon. He did not tell him that he was going to look through the footage of the dumpster cam to see if he could figure out exactly when the new owner of Snarkey's threw out the unsold slices. Or that he might wander down the street where Cassie Byzinski lived, in case she was out on her porch or something. He did not explain that the first day of vacation, by definition, had to include a significant number of gaming hours. Or that the whole point of that hallowed first day was that it not *have* much of a plan but be spent soaking in the gloriousness of no one telling you what to do every forty-two minutes.

Principal Deming was not Quagmire's friend, which Deming had proved at least 153 times this year, the last of which was Tuesday, and Quag did not feel the need to stop in the hall after the last bell of the last class on the last day of school and have a little chat about his summer plans. Nope. Quagmire had a policy about stupid questions: Just because you decided to ask one did not obligate him to answer.

But now, here it is, the first full day of vacation and not even ten a.m., and the whole day is already up in flames. Because his mom is having one of her spinning days. Which beats the crap out of one of her crying days, but means that she'd waked him up at 6:33 in the morning to say, "Happy summer vacation and tell me the best thing that's happened for you this year and, here, I bought you a sausage biscuit." And Quag had been feeling so good, chilling there in bed with a huge, warm sausage biscuit in a beautifully greasy bag sitting on his chest, that he'd actually told her about the best thing that had happened that year. Told her about the time that he'd taken over the sound booth for the Jazz Lab concert, and about the band kids shaving their heads to protest budget cuts and everything that had gone on that night.

And that had been a bad call. An enormous strategic mistake. He should have known better. How had he missed the signs that she was spinning? He would have laid low if he'd picked up on that.

Because now she's spinning on the head-shaving thing—even though that isn't the point of the story—laughing too loud and crowding him in the hall as she follows him down to the kitchen. "Why would they do that" while he eats his sausage biscuit. "That one girl had such pretty hair" while he tries to play through a level of *Forza*. And "It will take forever to grow out" through the door of the bathroom, for crying out loud, and on and on and on.

It's a Saturday, so this is all he's going to hear all day and maybe tomorrow too, because when his mom isn't okay—and she isn't okay today—these spins can go on for who knows how long.

And Quag can't do it. Not today.

Not on the first day of summer vacation.

He ducks out the front, closing the door on "So why didn't you shave yours," and sprints down the alley beside the apartments in case his mom tries to follow. He hops the fence and turns down Laurel toward the lake. Rain starts by the time he gets to Clark's Fish Fry—of course it does. But it is no way going to be worth it to go back for a jacket. And it's a warm end-of-June rain anyway. The kind of welcome rain that takes the mugginess down a notch and clears the tourists out of the thin strip of grass along the lake.

He can see a family piling into a red SUV and a couple of others squeezing into the gazebo trying to stay dry as he slows down, crosses Lake Street, and comes under the arch that leads into the park. A slightly disreputable-looking duck, a tuft of down sticking up from its head, stops nibbling on a bush and falls into step with Quag, rocking along beside him as though it has been waiting for him. Man, ducks look stupid when they walk. Probably get no respect from anyone just because they look so stupid, waddling along like that, duck butt swinging.

The rain is picking up now, slapping against his face and arms, popping against the sidewalk in a way that makes getting out of the rain something he wants to do. He comes around the stone wall of the World War memorial (built when they thought there was only going to be one, apparently), duck still waddling along beside him—one, two, one, two—and stops under the little overhang above the plaque of names. He slides down against the wall. The duck stops too, looking out at the lake.

What is up with this duck?

But okay, he can sit here in the wet with a weird duck.

He watches the rain turn the whole surface of the lake into a spiky sheet of leaping gray drops. He feels the raised bronze names of dead guys pressing into his back. The duck waddles the few steps to the little sunken fountain in front of the monument and starts swimming.

No way. A whole lake, and this dumb duck is going to swim laps in a tiny cement pond. Around and around and around, little legs going like he's getting somewhere. Quag watches the lake and the duck and the rain and the dark, low clouds.

His mom is getting worse.

TWO

Quag likes to look at the footage from the dumpster cam right before he goes to bed. Kind of like some people watch a favorite TV show. Or listen to white noise to get to sleep.

It's always the same thing—the frame filled with the dumpster and a battered picnic table where the workers from Snarkey's Pizza take their breaks. A branch of the maple tree that has forced its way up through the pavement in the alley between Quag's house and Snarkey's sometimes dips in and out of the camera frame when the wind blows.

Even the characters repeat. A blank frame, and then there will be the delivery driver who looks like Legolas, if Legolas had shaved the left side of his elf head down to stubble, wore what looked like a silver-coated booger dangling from his right nostril, and liked to stand on top of picnic tables doing tai chi. Or there will be the girl with all the braids who reads an organic chemistry textbook during breaks as if it's a novel where something big is always about to go down—focused, her long fingers turning the pages and her eyes flicking to the top of the next page as it turns over. Or the kid with the floppy hair who puts his head down on his arms and is immediately, completely asleep, out cold through his whole break, until his phone buzzes him awake. Same stories, same characters, over and over and over.

Still. Quag hasn't learned what he set up the camera to find out: Where are the unsold pizza slices going? Last year, the guy who'd been running the place for as long as Quag had been living here used to wait until all the employees were gone, then chuck a box or two of perfectly good slices, sometimes still hot, into the dumpster. But recently, he'd been replaced by this new guy—younger, jittery, all quick movements and impatience—and the pizza no longer appeared at 10:15.

Is he taking it home himself? Giving it to the people who work there? Trashing it at a different time?

It's been two pizza-less weeks, and Quag is about to give up on the whole thing. But it's kind of a habit now to watch the cam feed, so he scrolls through anyway. Mostly empty. But then he watches Legolas smoking something that doesn't seem to be a standard-issue cigarette. Notes how far Chemistry Girl has read in her book. Watches Floppy Hair Guy snore.

He's about to shut it down when he sees, just in the corner of the frame, a movement. Someone who must have been sitting on the back steps of the pizzeria stands, and for a second, Quag sees some short, dark hair riffling in the wind. And an ear.

It is a perfect ear. An ear that he knows the exact proportions of, all the curves and turnings, because he sat next to the owner of that ear in a sound booth for two and a half months last year.

Cassie was here?

He rewinds. Pauses. He feels weirdly skittery about this ear. He is not at all sleepy anymore.

What is Cassie Byzinski doing on his dumpster cam? Did she just happen to be wandering past earlier today? Or is she working next door at the pizza place?

So that's how Quag ends up in Snarkey's three times in the next two days. First time, he asks for a take-out menu, even though everybody knows you can look that up on your phone. Second time, he reads the notices on the Community News for You bulletin board inside the door, with the guy at the register eyeballing him the whole time. Quag isn't the sort of kid people like hanging out in their shops. Third time, it's busy, and Quag has to buy a Coke—which is the cheapest thing in the place—out of the refrigerated case so he'll have time to check out the hectic scene behind the counter. He listens to the voices in back of the partition calling out, "Two pepperoni for delivery" and the answering "Two pepp!" But it's never the right face behind the counter and never the right voice beyond the partition, and it's kind of annoying to be buying Coke when what Quag wants is pizza. But his mom won't get paid for another couple of days still, if she gets paid at all.

It's time to redirect the dumpster cam to be the back-door-so-anybody-that-comes-or-goes-will-be-on-the-loop cam. This is not the easiest adjustment to make. First, because Mrs. Durock, who lives in the first-floor apartment, makes it her mission in life to report pretty much everything Quag does, up to and including breathing, to both his mom and the landlord. *That boy upstairs is existing again. I want this stopped immediately.*

Second, because Quag has to climb over the railing of the old fire escape, hang on to the handrail, and swing one foot out to rest on a black iron hook sticking out from the wall, which holds a hanging pot of some stupid-looking, frilly, hot pink flowers belonging to Mrs. Durock. This puts him spread-eagled against the wall, practically kissing the grungy siding. Then, once he's steadied himself there for a minute, he will stretch as far as he can, balancing on one foot on that hook, and reach around the corner of the building to fiddle with the cam he stuck onto the siding with a blob of J-B Weld. If the guy who built this house hadn't been so stingy with the windows (there are exactly two on each floor, one facing the front street and one facing the gravel parking strip behind the apartments), Quag's life would be easier.

Quag waits by the front window until Mrs. Durock's beige Buick pulls out, then heads for the Emergency Use Only door at the far end of the hall. He climbs out to the fire escape, checks to make sure no one is in the yard behind Snarkey's, and scrambles over the railing, wedging one sneaker between the posts and swinging the other out to land on the iron hook. And Quag is leaning way out, balanced, one hand still gripping the handrail, the other arm stretched, ready to reach around the corner and tweak the angle of the camera, when he hears a voice.

"Quag?"

Quag knows that voice like he'd known that ear. He slams back to the fire escape, as far out of the arc of the camera as he can get. The frilly flowers swing wildly on their hook. And Quag knows beyond all knowing that as soon as he twists around, he will see, standing below him on the back steps of Snarkey's, under the striped green-and-white awning, Cassie Byzinski, running her fingers through her hair.

Where did she come from?

She looks up at him, eyebrows raised. "What are you doing?" she asks.

Of course that's what she asks.

Quag's sneakers squeak as he squidges his feet around so that he is at least facing Cassie. He tries to figure the angles from where she stands. Can she see the cam from there? He's pretty sure not. Unless she walks out to the picnic table or something.

So that can't happen.

"Quag?" Cassie asks again.

"Uh, you can see the lake from here," says Quag.

Stupid. Especially since he had been facing away from the lake when she first asked. But infinitely better than the truth, which now seems weird and stalkerish and like one of those things he should go all out to keep anyone, anywhere, from ever finding out.

A couple of those little birds that show up wherever people drop crumbs from sandwiches flit down to the picnic table.

"Also birds," says Quag. "You can see a lot of birds from up here."

Cassie wrinkles up her forehead. "Are you a birder?"

Quagmire Tiarello learned long ago that when you bluff, you bluff big. "Absolutely," he says.

Cassie seems unconvinced. "Like you have a life list and everything?"

Quag has no idea what a life list is. Quag does not exactly know what a birder is. Something to do with birds, apparently. Quag has no idea what kind of birds those two grayish-brown things on the picnic table are.

"Doesn't everyone have a life list?" he asks.

"Huh," says Cassie. "My Aunt Becca is a birder, but I never really thought of you as the birder type."

"I feel like people have some pretty inflexible stereotypes about birders," says Quag.

"Okay," says Cassie.

Quag's toes are starting to cramp from trying to cling to the narrow lip of the fire escape platform outside the railing. He would not mind loosening up his fingers either.

"So, I'm on my break," says Cassie. "And I was just going to take a quick walk along that path behind the hardware store. The one along the creek. Want to come?"

Quag does want to come. But to get back over the railing (which, now that he looks at it, is quite a bit higher than it really needs to be just to keep someone from pitching over the edge), he will have to kind of shinny up the posts until he can balance on his stomach on the creaky rail and then schlump himself over, all in front of Cassie.

"There's all kinds of birds down there too," says Cassie. "That trail is full of birds."

Perfect. Couldn't be better. Birds. Because now he's some birder with some birder list that Cassie knows more about than he does. And if the first rule of the bluff is bluff big, the second is to make sure you can back it up. And Quag, clinging to a rusty railing above Cassie's head, is all kinds of aware that he is in no position to do that right now. One of the things he likes about Cassie is that she's smart, that she figures things out. That she calls people's bluffs.

He does not want her calling this one.

"Can't," Quag says. "Dentist appointment. Two cavities."

"Ouch," says Cassie. "Sorry."

"Yeah," says Quag. "Me too."

And he is sorry. Sorry that of all the stinking hours in the stinking world, he tried to tweak the cam during this one. Sorry that his toes might never uncurl. Sorry that his knuckles are turning white while he and Cassie chat about stupid birds and stupid nonexistent dentists. But, most of all, sorry that Cassie Byzinski, with a little wave, is taking a walk on a beautiful summer day, and he is not going with her.

BIRDS

There are some seriously weird birds in the world—birds with faces that look like freakish dinosaurs, birds with their knees on backward, birds that look like they're wearing bad toupees, birds with geeked-out dance moves. Quagmire Tiarello knows all of this because, even though it's summer vacation, thanks to that meet-up with Cassie Byzinski yesterday, he is spending this morning doing research on stupid birds.

Also, those gray birds on the picnic table were sparrows. Probably. Which doesn't help as much as you'd think, since there are about fifty kinds of sparrows even if you limit them to the ones that hang out in the state of New York.

Sparrows aren't even from here. Some guy in the 1850s decided to bring a few over from Europe to eat the caterpillars by his house in New York City because what could go wrong, right? So from there, they took over North America and are the mafia overlords of Snarkey's picnic table. The internet says they mostly eat seeds (so, sorry, dude who brought them over to eat caterpillars, wrong bird), but the ones at Snarkey's fight over pizza crusts. So they'll take their seeds ground and with extra cheese, apparently.

Also, they'll eat Cheetos when they can get them. One was in a serious smackdown with a Cheeto this morning. Could not tell who was winning. Both the sparrow and the Cheeto were putting up a good fight.

THREE

This birder thing is going to be a major hassle. By eleven, Quag gives up. Too many birds. He is going to enjoy the rest of this day. Against all odds.

He heads out to the park. He's met at the arch by the duck.

Perfect. Couldn't be better.

There are signs in the park saying not to feed the ducks—something about people food making them fat or something. (News flash: It does that to people too.) What the signs don't bother to mention is that if you aren't paying too much attention to signs, and you happen one day to give a stupid-looking duck a quarter of a peanut butter sandwich, the duck will take it as a vow of eternal friendship. Start following you around the park every time you show up.

Which makes you look as stupid as the duck.

Quag walks faster, trying to put some distance between himself and the duck. The duck breaks into a trot-waddle. So now it looks like he's being chased by a duck.

Perfect.

Quag's phone buzzes. He ignores it. Probably his mom. Who he has spent the whole morning dodging. She usually sleeps till way late on days when she's not at work. But this week she hasn't been sleeping hardly at all that Quag can tell. Staying up later than he is, still up (or getting up, he isn't sure) before he does. And she's in one of her talk, talk, talk, talk, talk moods. Which Quag can handle for about half a day, and then he has to bail, or he'll talk, talk back, and she'll take it wrong, and there'll be yelling. Then Mrs. Durock will show up at their door, which totally isn't worth the hassle.

Quag had spent this morning on the roof outside his bedroom window looking up random bird facts on his phone to avoid the fight with his mom, but it gets kind of hot up there on a sunny day. So he's been kicking around town. He stopped in at Jake's house, but Jake's mom said he and Nick were off at some music camp. And Mac spends the month after school gets out visiting his dad's family in Brazil every year. So no one's around. Thus the move to the park.

If it's his mom on his phone, she will start her cycle of text, text, call, call, leave a message, text again, email (as if anyone uses email anymore), text, text, text, text, text. But it's a beautiful sunny day. Quag has five bucks in his pocket for a legitimate, non-dumpster slice from Snarkey's, which will give him a perfect excuse to stop by later. He is not going to deal with his mom. It's the fourth day of summer vacation. Not required to deal with reality on the fourth day.

He settles down in his war monument spot and looks at the lake. Someone is out there in an orange kayak slicing along, paddling like going fast is her whole purpose in life. Quag's phone does its "You have not looked at your last text" reminder buzz.

Maybe it isn't his mom. Her usual thing is one text every seven seconds. He fishes his phone out of his pocket.

Cassie.

Cassie Byzinski.

He watches the orange kayak skimming along the surface of the lake.

Cassie Byzinski. Who wants to know, *"What are you doing this summer?"*

Hanging out with a duck, thinks Quag. Like some birder loser. He texts back.

Why?

Got an idea
If you're going to be around
Are you?

Probably

He'll be around. They almost never go anywhere during the summer.

Where are you now?

Lakeside park

Where in lakeside park

War memorial

Be right there

Quag stares at his phone for a minute, to see if any further clarification is coming. Then, when nothing appears, he wonders if he should text something back. Or has he waited too long, and now it would be stupid? Cassie doesn't seem to need his input on this.

He looks over at the duck, who is investigating the wrapper from a peanut butter cup caught in the bottom branches of a bush. Peanut butter must be like duck cocaine.

"Cassie's coming," he tells the duck. The duck finishes worrying the wrapper, eats a leaf, and waddles off toward the fountain.

"She really is," Quag yells after the duck.

The duck climbs in without looking back and starts his daily laps.

It doesn't take Cassie long to get to the park. She comes across the grass and drops down beside him. "What's with the duck?"

"He does that," says Quag. They watch the duck swimming his little circles around the fountain.

"What's his name?" asks Cassie.

"Clyde," says Quag.

Cassie tips her head and considers. "What's his middle name?" she asks.

"Doesn't have one."

"All ducks have middle names. Or at least middle initials." Cassie takes a snack pack of pretzel nibs out of her hoodie pocket and offers Quag some. They sit, crunching pretzels and watching Clyde. "Maybe it's Q," says Cassie. "Clyde Q. Duck. Or Clyde Q. Duck, the Third."

"Could be," Quag allows. What does Cassie want to talk to him about? Probably not ducks, with or without initials. But if he asks her, and she tells him, will she leave then?

He kind of doesn't want her to leave. Kind of wants her to stay here, sitting close enough that when she reaches for another pretzel, the sleeve of her hoodie brushes his arm. Kind of wants to maybe sit here all day, with the June sun on his face and Cassie's hair swirling around in the breeze so that she keeps trying to tuck it back behind her ears, even though it's still too short to stay there. Maybe they'll just sit here until the whole summer goes by, boats coming in and out, until the sun and the stars have spun around them a hundred times. Watching a duck.

Quag wouldn't mind.

"Cottonwood," says Cassie.

"What?"

"The little fluffs," she says, pointing. "Floating all over in the air. They're from the cottonwood trees over by the elementary school playground."

"How do you know they're not from dandelions?"

"They're not," Cassie insists. "Because (a) dandelions are over. So last month. And (b) because they look different. Dandelion fluffs are like these little crowns with the seed hanging below. But cottonwood fluffs are littler and floatier. Also, they go up more, like they don't weigh anything at all. But dandelions always look like they're headed for a crash landing." Now that Cassie has pointed them out, Quag can see the cottonwood fluffs everywhere—floating through the air, caught in the grass, skimming in rafts over the surface of the lake.

"Maybe they're duck fluffs," says Quagmire, just because he wants her to keep talking. He nods toward Clyde gently circling the fountain.

"Nope," says Cassie. "To get that many duck fluffs, a duck would have to explode."

"Could have happened," says Quag. "Central New York is lousy with exploding ducks."

"Right," says Cassie. She finishes the last pretzel nib, shakes the salt in the bottom of the package out onto her tongue, and wads up the wrapper. She hops up from where she's sitting. Looks down at him. "Hey, so are you doing anything this summer, or do you want to help some of us do a radio play? We want to do some cool stuff with the sound," she says.

What's a radio play? Quag isn't sure. Like a podcast before there were podcasts? Or TV without pictures? Seems kind of dumb.

"Lily's out of town most of this summer. So I need someone else for our ArtCamp team at the Y. There are kids coming from all over," says Cassie. "Foster Lake Middle, Westside. It's not just our school."

Big deal.

But there is Cassie with the sun gleaming against her hair and her hands on her hips and that kind of intense look she gives you whenever she asks you a question—a look like whatever your answer is matters—and Quag can still feel the sun and the stars and the planets whirling around them.

"Sure," he says.

Because how bad can it be? Because it's Cassie asking. Because sometimes it gets boring in the summer when everyone else in the world seems to be at camp or on vacation all the time. And because ever since he got kicked off drama crew for taking over the sound booth during the Jazz Lab protest concert, he's really missed running a soundboard.

BIRDS: AGAIN

There are birds everywhere. It's actually starting to freak Quag out a little. He walks past a bush, and a bunch of fat little yellow-and-black birds come flying out in this bizarre bobbing way that reminds Quag of bumblebees or something. When he woke up this morning, he could hear like fifteen birds totally going at it. When he walked out the door, there was this huge shiny black bird sitting on the railing of the apartment building looking at Quag like, "How dare you walk down these steps." And that duck. Which finds him every single time he goes to the park.

Have there always been this many birds around, and he didn't notice? Or is this some sort of freaky curse he brought on by lying about being a birder?

FOUR

The YMCA is not someplace Quag hangs out. He's pretty much avoided it since fourth grade, which was the year his mom signed him up for the swim team because the counselor at school said he needed "socialization." Like he was a puppy who kept biting the other puppies, or something.

Swim team was run by a woman with a booming voice who yelled, "Stay in your lane. All right, people, dig, dig, dig," through a megaphone. Stupid. When, partway through practice, Quag, bored with all the back-and-forth, dived down to see if he could touch the drain, the coach had a complete meltdown, and the "stay in your lane" chant went into an every-six-second loop as she walked along the side of the pool beside Quag.

And "stay in your lane" so you could cover the same ground (or water) over and over for no reason except to see if you could cover it faster than someone else seemed like the sort of thing grown-ups who have stopped thinking about their lives might do, but not a nine-year-old with better options. Quag lasted twenty minutes, until it was pretty clear that this back, forth, back, forth, back, forth was all that was going to happen, and then he climbed out of the pool and headed out the emergency exit, the coach yelling, "Get right back here, young man," after him until he was outside, and the hubbub of alarm bells and voices echoing in a concrete cube was whooshed into silence by the closing door.

Sunshine. Freedom.

He hadn't been back since.

But this radio play thing is at the Y, and when Quag asked, "Why there?" Cassie said, "Because ArtCamp, duh," in a way that definitely made it seem like he should know all about that. Not wanting to put himself more solidly in the duh category, he didn't ask any more questions.

So this morning he's headed up past Bainbridge Park to the YMCA. A pickup-truck-size ARTCAMP banner screams across the side of the building with a huge green arrow pointing down to an open door that does make the whole thing seem kind of duh. Under the sign, a woman with long gray hair and a pointy nose sits at a table. "Middle school or high school?" she asks, giving Quag a sharp look.

Quag's pretty sure he doesn't like this lady. He makes her wait.

"Which grade will you be going into this September?" she clarifies, impatiently.

Count to five. Watch her get annoyed. "Ninth," says Quag.

"So, that's high school," she says, shuffling her lists. Quag feels the duh hanging in the air between them. The duh makes him mad. So, when she puts out a hand and says, "Forms," even though it's clear he doesn't have any forms to give her, he just looks at her. Pointy-nose lady sighs and hauls out a stack of forms from one of her piles. "Bring these in tomorrow. You'll work with Mr. Knudrick. Through the door, turn left, room at the end of the hall. Good luck."

Does "good luck" refer to finding the room, working with Mr. Knudrick, or the experience of ArtCamp in general? Which is definitely feeling like something a kid who is fourteen and has better things to do with his life might want to pass on about now. Tell Pointy Nose that she can keep her duh and her forms and her good luck.

But then Cassie comes swinging across the grass, and Quag forgets to walk away.

"Oh, good. You're here," Cassie says, as if that had been in question. He'd said he'd be here. And then she says, "Hey, Ms. Alvarez," to the duh lady, who doesn't ask her which grade she's going into, doesn't ask her for forms, just goes all smiley and calls out, "Caaaaassie!"

Like because Cassie Byzinski turned up, sitting at this table with a cheap, yellow plastic tablecloth and a pile of clipboards all morning is totally worth it. Quag's weirdly jealous that there is someone else who feels that way about Cassie being here.

She burrows under her table to pull out a box and hands it to Cassie. "Your clipboard is in there, key to the supply closet is in the envelope. You can pick up your budget at the main desk when your group is ready for it. Have fun, young lady."

Have fun.

Not good luck.

Quag follows Cassie down the hall. An annoying number of

kids are milling around. It feels like the hall at school between classes. Quag just escaped from the hall at school five days ago. This had better not be anything like school.

Quag only knows a few of the kids, but all of them seem to know Cassie. Greetings ring out up and down the length of the hall. When they get to the end, Cassie shoulders through a door, holding it open for him. An assortment of mismatched furniture is scattered around a room. A tall girl with a long black ponytail is draped over a poofy, yellow beanbag chair. She looks up from her phone as they come in.

"Rhia!" Cassie greets her.

"Hey," says Rhia, unfolding herself and rising from the beanbag. "I was just texting you." She looks like someone who plays hockey. Or weightlifts. Or is a judo champion. Something.

"Where's Mikey? Where's Jax?" asks Cassie.

Rhia rolls her eyes. "Jax is reprogramming a Magic Eight Ball to give out Shakespearean insults."

"Why?" asks Cassie.

Rhia shrugs. "Because he's Jax."

"And Mikey?"

"He's with Jax," says Rhia. "Because he's Mikey. I told them to get over here. They're coming."

"Great," says Cassie. "This is Quag."

Rhia turns to Quag. "Hey," she says. "Rhia Suani. You're the one who did the concert takeover with the Jazz Lab."

It's a statement, not a question, so Quag doesn't answer.

"Nice," says Rhia. "I wasn't there. I'm from Westside. But I heard about it." She glances down at her phone. "Ah. They're here."

Two boys bang through the door, laughing and talking. One is a short, roundish, curly-headed kid with a surprisingly low voice for his size. Like some voice-over guy from a television commercial is walking around wearing Harry Potter glasses and Crocs in the Y hallway. The other kid is tall, skinny, has short dreads with bleached tips, and carries a cardboard box brimming with dismembered electronics.

"Check it out!" The round kid reaches into the box and tosses a Magic 8 Ball to Rhia, who catches it in one hand and shakes it.

"'Be gone, whey-faced chatbot'?" reads Rhia.

"'Chatbot'?" says Cassie. "I thought you were making a *Shakespearean* insult generator."

"Everybody has those," says the skinny kid.

In what world does everybody have those?

"He made a Shakespeare and modern mash-up insult generator," explains the round kid. "It's genius." He takes the Magic 8 Ball from Rhia and hands it to Quagmire. "Try it."

This is a really smiley kid. Quag's not sure what he thinks of this kid. But he takes the ball and shakes it. Cassie leans over to look. "'Fie, selfie-loving clack-dish,'" she reads. "Mikey, what does that even mean?"

The round kid, Mikey apparently, grins even bigger and drops into the beanbag chair. "No idea," he admits. "But it is *definitely* an insult. You can just tell."

Cassie takes the ball from Quag and shakes it. She turns the screen toward the kid with the dreads. "Now it just says 'Pigeon.'"

"An insult in either age," says the kid, shrugging.

"Wow, Jax," says Rhia. "A little harsh on pigeons."

"I call it how I see it," says Jax.

Cassie smiles and sets the ball back into the box. "Hey, everyone. You know how Lily's family took her out of town this month?" Mikey makes an exaggerated sad face, lower lip trembling. "So, this is Quagmire Tiarello. He's going to step in and work with us this year."

"Wait! What?" says Mikey, turning toward Quag. "Like THE Quagmire Tiarello? Like the man, the myth, the legend? *That* Quagmire Tiarello?" He scrambles out of the beanbag and drops to one knee. "I grovel at your feet."

"Stop, Mikey," says Rhia. "Now you're being weird."

Quag is with Rhia on this one.

"Weird is my brand," says Mikey, undaunted. But he gets up from the floor.

Jax nods once at Quag. "Nice work on that takeover in the spring," he says. "We all saw the video. Wish I could have seen that one live, though. The video quality wasn't the best, but it looked like it was epic."

It was epic.

Quag will still go on the internet sometimes and watch the video, even though the quality is pretty bad (Jax is right about that), just to remember what it felt like to be there that night. And probably ArtCamp won't be like that. Maybe nothing will ever be quite like that. But there will be a soundboard. And there will be

Cassie. And even though it feels like he's fallen into some world where everything is just a little off from normal, these kids are at least not boring.

So he's in.

FIVE

First day is Scavenger Hunt Day at ArtCamp. This is apparently a yearly thing. Your team gets a clue and a task, and you have to walk into town and do whatever random thing is on your card—"Perform 'Twinkle, Twinkle, Little Star' with hand motions or interpretive dance elements"—for whatever shop owner your clue leads you to. And then that shop owner gives you the next clue, and so on, till one team gets to the fifth clue and the grand prize.

Whatever.

But everyone's trash-talking and completely into it. They're weird kids, these drama kids. They get into stuff.

So they're running all over the little downtown, and though it feels strange to be doing things with a group like this, and he's not loving some of the tasks—"Ask for the next clue as if you are a frog chorus"—really?—it's not too bad. If you like that kind of stuff.

And Quag's pretty sure his team might be ahead—Rhia can run like nobody's business and usually has the whole thing set up, so they only have to do the last bit when they come puffing in. So when Quag is handed the final clue, and he unfolds it and realizes it's for Snarkey's, which he happens to know a shortcut to, he's almost sure they'll win.

But then there's a problem. Because as they're leaving the shop, Quag's mom is marching down the sidewalk toward them, carrying her big yellow purse. She hasn't seen them yet, but any second, she will. And for some reason, Quag immediately knows that he doesn't want that to happen. That it *can't* happen.

He ducks into the next shop down, still holding the clue. "Here?" asks Cassie, reaching for the slip of paper. "Wait, let me see it." But she follows him in, and the other kids follow her.

Mikey jumps and grabs the paper out of Quag's hand. "This isn't it!" Mikey bends over the card. "It says 'cheese' on the clue card!"

Quag scans the shop. "This shop sells seven different colors of lava lamps. How is it possible to be more cheesy than that?"

"The clue also says pie," counters Jax, looking over Mikey's shoulder.

This one takes a bit of quick thinking. "The address," says Quag. "Didn't you notice the address?" His arms are out. He's selling this. "314 Lake Street? Like 3.1415, like mathematics, like pi, like Pi Day, all that?"

"It was? Really?" Mikey is starting to waver.

But not Rhia. "You're overthinking this by a lot, Tiarello. It's obviously for Snarkey's."

Which it is. But just as Rhia is saying this, Quag sees his mom march into view in front of the window of the shop. He wills her not to stop. Not to look in the window. Don't look, don't look, don't look.

And she doesn't. She walks past.

Why is she not at work right now?

"Quag, it's definitely Snarkey's," says Cassie.

To make sure they have enough distance between them and his mom, Quag pretends to think that over. "Isn't that awfully obvious?" he asks.

Cassie puffs out an exasperated breath. "They've all been obvious!" she says. "Doing the improv thing when you get there is the important part, not figuring out some complicated clue. Let's go!" And now the group is on the move, and Quag has one more thing he has to manage so that this day doesn't crash. He has to make sure the group turns right instead of left to get to Snarkey's. Because they could go either way from here. And his mom is left.

He hops over a low display table to get in front of everyone— earning a "Hey!" from the shop clerk—leads them out the door, turns them right, and hurries off down the street without looking left once.

Though he wants to look. To be sure. But people can feel it when you look at them; he knows it. And he can't risk it. Can't risk the voice calling his name. Does not want the voice calling his name.

They make it to Snarkey's without seeing his mom. But another group has beaten them there and is hoisting an extra-large pizza with everything on it—the Pie-a-Palooza—over their heads in victory as Cassie's group tumbles in the door. So they're in second place, and for that, the guy behind the counter announces that they've won a large order of Cheesy Chunks.

It's a good bet that whoever named those failed their marketing class. Jax is side-eyeing Quag like he's thinking the same thing, which makes them both laugh out loud. But the chunks themselves are actually okay. They're hot, they're filling, there's a ton of cheese, and the dipping sauces are good. So even though Quag has to take all kinds of crap over the fact that the store he pulled them into actually had the address of 211 (Rhia looked on the way out) and "How is that pi, Quag, how is that even mathematical in any way," and even though it's a bummer that they lost out on the Pie-a-Palooza, which is the second-best pizza on the menu (Quag and Cassie and Mikey all agree that Pepperoni Paparazzi is the best), Quag's okay with it. Because they don't see his mom anywhere all the way back to the Y.

He feels bad about avoiding her. He feels like doing that makes him like all the jerk people in town who always speed up and get really busy with their phones when she's walking by. But there's another part of him that is just relieved.

BIRDS: DISTRACTION

There's this one kind of bird called a killdeer (which makes it sound like it's some kind of major hunter or something, but that's not it at all, so Quag's not sure what the deal is with the name). Anyway, the bird lays its eggs on the ground. Seems like asking for trouble. But then if a fox or something gets too close to the nest, this bird breaks into all-out-drama-queen mode, acting like its wing is majorly broken and fluttering around like, "Oh no, I am completely wigging out here, because there is a *fox*, and the fox is going to *eat* me, and I'm trying to get away, but I *can't* get away." On the YouTube video Quag watched, it totally looks like the bird is toast.

But actually, it's a pretty smart bird. Because after it gets the fox to not notice the nest with all this thrashing and looking like it can only fly enough to barely stay out of the fox's mouth, and the fox is following it and following it, always thinking it's two seconds from chowing down, then the bird's all like, "And now I will make a fox look like a total thickskull," and it magically heals itself and flies off. If birds can laugh, Quag's pretty sure this bird was laughing as it did this little "Later, sucker" swoop away from the fox.

SIX

"I have a brilliant idea for game of the day," Mikey is saying as Quag walks into ArtCamp the next morning. "Choose a movie title, and by only changing one word in the title, change it from a drama to a comedy, or a comedy to a drama."

"Example," says Rhia, rolling her shoulders. "I don't get it."

"Okay," says Mikey. "So. You take the movie *Great Expectations*, right? And it's like a drama, but if you change the title to *Great Expectorations*, then it's a comedy. See?" Mikey is cracking himself up.

Everyone stares at Mikey.

"Why?" asks Jax.

"Because!" Mikey gestures grandly. "Now Miss Havisham is just sitting around in her wedding dress spitting, see? Ptooey. Ptooey. *Great Expectorations*, right? Total comedy."

"Okay," says Rhia. "That is probably the worst possible example you could have even given."

"It's brilliant!" protests Mikey, incensed.

"No," says Cassie. "Because (a) only three people in the world have seen that movie, so we don't even know what you're spoofing, and (b) only one person in the world"—she points to Mikey—"knows that expectorating means spitting."

"Not true!" Mikey protests. "Everyone knows that!" He turns to the group for support.

"Nope," says Rhia.

Jax shakes his head sadly as he wraps electrical tape around a set of wires. "Nobody, Mikey. Nobody but you."

Quag knows. But no way is he admitting that at this point.

"Concept is solid though," says Rhia. "Just pick a movie made in this century. And leave the thesaurus at home."

"Yeah, the concept is genius," says Cassie.

Mikey is immediately returned to full good humor by this. "Isn't it, though? I thought of it this morning while I was eating Lucky Charms. I was like, 'What if it was called Lucky Harms'?"

Yeah, what if? Mikey is a goofball. Being around him is like having real-time, live access to the workings of a really strange brain. But he's okay.

"Also," says Mikey, "next Tuesday is my birthday. Don't forget."

"Nobody is going to forget, Mikey," says Cassie.

"Because you are going to remind us every twenty minutes until Tuesday," says Rhia, cracking her knuckles.

"We've got to present our project to Mr. Knudrick no later than tomorrow," says Cassie. "We need to get going. Mikey, did you finish the scripts?"

"You know it." Mikey thunks a stack of papers down on a chair.

"Cool. So Mikey and Rhia are acting this year. I'm directing. Jax is our soundman."

What?

Quag feels a seismic murmur run down his center. The murmur becomes a shiver. Shale starts to fall from cliffs in Quag's chest. He can feel the rumble of larger rocks coming loose somewhere deep inside.

He'd just assumed. That it was obvious. He'd assumed that he, Quagmire Tiarello, would be the soundman.

Rhia says out loud what Quag, trying to deal with an internal 8.2 temblor, hasn't quite gotten to thinking yet. "So, what's Quag got, then?"

Cassie looks over at Quag with a smile. "Quag is here as our Foley guy."

Foley guy?

What even is that?

Before Quag can get himself together enough to ask, an announcement comes on, and they're headed off down the hall for an all-groups meeting with this Mr. Knudrick person. Mr. Knudrick turns out to be a young guy wearing dark jeans and bright yellow glasses that make him look like he walked out of some hipster coffee shop.

Wow. The man is seriously upbeat about everything. It's going to be a great year, and he's so glad to see them, so excited to work with them. He makes Ms. Morales, Quag's most exhaustingly positive teacher from last year, look like she was depressed by comparison.

But Quag does not care that if your group has worked with Mr. Knudrick before (Rhia does a little fist pump here and then bumps knuckles with Jax), you can make your own rules and spend your budget how you want and pick out a project that you're interested in, rather than choosing from the list, as long as you run it by Mr. Knudrick first. Quag does not care that next week, there will be a Show Your Stuff session in front of the group to get feedback. Nope. Quag does not care about the Big Show ("for all your many friends and fans") after four weeks.

What Quag cares about is the soundboard. He has to talk to Cassie about the soundboard. Isn't that what she'd been talking about when she met him at the park? Like when she said they wanted to do some cool stuff with the sound? Soundboard!

But when they'd gotten to the auditorium where this meeting is being held, Mikey had plunked himself down on one side of Cassie, and Rhia, who keeps leaning over and saying things that make Cassie smile, sat down on the other side. Somehow, even Jax ended up between Quag and Cassie.

Quag slides down in his seat and pulls his phone out to look up that Foley thing Cassie said he's supposed to do. He spells it wrong the first time and comes up with some website about an oxygen canister, then a law firm in the next town over. Then he finally hits "Foley Artist," which, apparently, is somebody who does sound effects for movies. Or radio shows, he guesses.

There's a video of some guy chopping a cabbage in half with a machete, though Quag doesn't know what that's about, because he's looking at all of this with the sound off. Quag doesn't think the "good luck" lady at the registration table is going to be all over people showing up at the Y with machetes. Though that might be the one good thing about this. *Let me through with my machete. It's a Foley thing.*

Whatever. Dumb job. Why not find sound files? Why not use plug-ins? Why not run all of this through the soundboard? So much better.

The meeting is still going full tilt. Perfect. Now there's a group cheer. Couldn't be better. Quag is not feeling it. But, finally, this Knudrick guy is doing a set of dance steps and a bow, and it's over, and people are spilling out of their seats and heading for the door.

Quag moves closer to Cassie. Soundboard, soundboard, soundboard, he wants to say, but all the kids from the auditorium are walking in a noisy crowd down the hall, and he doesn't want to discuss this in front of the whole camp.

Now they're out the big front doors of the Y, and everyone's peeling off to hop in waiting cars, or get on a bike, in Rhia's case. Cassie starts off down the sidewalk. Quag hurries to catch up.

SEVEN

"Hey," Quag says as he falls into step with Cassie.

"What's up?" says Cassie, putting her hands in the pockets of her hoodie. You'd think summer would be too warm for a hoodie. But Cassie wears this thing almost every single day. It's made of a light blue, T-shirt kind of fabric though, so maybe it's not hot. Who knows.

"I thought I'd be running the soundboard," says Quag.

"Nope," says Cassie, not even considering it. "Jax built the Y's soundboard out of parts. We didn't even used to have one. And it's a beast. The only person who knows how to work it is Jax."

Quag could figure it out. He figured out the school's board.

"You going this way?" asks Cassie. "I've got to walk down and pick up another roll of electrical tape for Jax from the hardware store."

Quag does some quick calculations. His mom, who actually went to work today (he watched the car pull out), won't be back for at least another hour even if there aren't a lot of rooms to clean. "I've got electrical tape at home," says Quag. "We can go by there and get it." Picking up something so obviously connected to running the soundboard as electrical tape seems like a good way to keep talking about this subject.

"Okay," says Cassie.

They turn and head across the outfield of the softball diamond.

"Foley artists are cool, Quag," says Cassie, partway across, clearly picking up on Quag's lack of enthusiasm.

Whatever the furthest thing from cool is, that's what Foley artists are.

"We're going to do it in real time too," said Cassie. "Like they used to on live radio."

Wow. His mistake. Infinitely cooler. Look at the people lining up for that. Nope.

They crunch through the infield. Cassie pulls a package of pretzel nibs out of her hoodie pocket. She opens it and offers one to Quag. He shakes his head. This conversation about the soundboard is not over.

They turn down Laurel. They walk past that stupid little ratball dog that always throws himself against the fence like this time he'll get free and murder Quag with his tiny teeth. Down past the house with a bunch of orange flowers planted to look like they've spilled out of a tipped-over wheelbarrow.

"Quag." Cassie has stopped in the middle of the sidewalk and is giving him her intense look. "You're not getting this. It's going to be this whole big thing." She's sweeping her arms out in front of her like she is creating something right here that she can see. "We don't have the big light and soundboard setup at the Y like we had at school. So we have to make it cool in other ways. Mikey had the idea of a radio play with live sound effects, which is cool but isn't visually interesting. But get this"—Cassie turns toward him, and her eyes are shining—"we'll have a couple of floods in the center of a dark stage. Rhia and Mikey will dress in black, white, and gray, so it's like an old black-and-white movie. Then toward the back of the stage on the side, you, in another flood, and you're dressed in black, and you're doing all the sound effects in real time with the audience watching you. See? I think you could be amazing."

This is the problem with Cassie. Whatever Cassie says while she's looking at him sounds better than it probably is, because Cassie is saying it. It's a problem.

Quag starts walking down the sidewalk again to give himself time to think. They turn onto Quag's street, passing Snarkey's on the way. Quag checks the apartment driveway for his mom's car. Not there. Good.

The railing going up the front steps to the apartment is rustier than he remembered though. And suddenly he's thinking about the bowl of Froot Loops he left on the table. The crusty microwave containers stacked in the sink. The ArtCamp forms, which his mom still hasn't filled out, on the counter. The laundry piled on a kitchen chair. Was it his mom's laundry? His? Were there boxers or mom underwear (which would be worse?) just sitting there in the middle of the kitchen?

"Hang on. I'll run up and get it," he says. He opens the outside door to the apartments and sprints up the old stairs. He pulls his key out and quickly unlocks the door.

Something's in front of the door as he tries to open it. Blocking it. He shoves at the door and sticks his head around to see what it is.

Flowers. In front of the door. Crammed into the garbage can from under the sink. Giant, blue, puffy flowers as big as Quag's head. Like the ones growing in the hedge in front of the library. *Are* they the flowers from in front of the library? Please don't let them be the flowers from in front of the library.

But they could be.

Quag can see, in his mind, his mom out there this morning, when he thought he'd talked her into going to work, maybe with the old bread knife with the cracked handle from the kitchen drawer. Hacking all those huge flowers off the hedge in front of the stone library on Lake Street. Like that was something any-body did. Piling them in her arms until the flowers were sliding, dropping, falling. But she would still be cutting, still be adding to the pile she couldn't hold. Because this is how it is when she finally tips over into definitely not okay. There is no such thing as enough.

He pushes past the blue flowers in the trash can, looks into the little kitchen. Flowers, everywhere. Orange flowers piled, broken, in a soft mound on the chipped table. Fat yellow roses dumped on the floor; spiky purple flowers slumped in the sink; a stem of what has to be Mrs. Durock's hot pink flowers hanging from the spigot; and the rest of them, torn up by the roots and chunks of dirt still clinging to them, scattered across the counter. An armload of maybe twenty cellophane-wrapped gas station roses are crammed on top of the refrigerator.

Quag stares at the kitchen.

A full-out spin. His mom's in a full-out, chaos-unleashed, major spin.

Quag hates a spin. Sometimes, it might start out good. Might seem like his mom is just celebrating a good day with a trip out to Foster's for huge, hot, thick hamburgers, grease and ketchup running down your wrists. And then they might move on to someplace interesting—a funky shop that only sells old license plates and car stuff, or a museum of quack doctoring—but pretty soon the car is going too fast and there are fifteen license plates from Texas and an enormous Valvoline sign shoved in the back seat and they're stopping at a convenience store to buy an armful of giant licorice whips and all of the hula-dancer bobbleheads on the shelves. Because now putting twenty-three of those on the dashboard is what's happening. But by then, Quag will just be trying to figure out how to get her back home, how to keep her from spending the rent, how to stop her from honking at the neighbors, how to get her in the house, how to call her in sick to work. How to hang on until it's over. And this time the spin, which he's felt creeping up on them for a week now, is starting with flowers.

Flowers.

Quag hears someone on the stairs behind him. Cassie. He tries to close the door. But he hears her breath catch, right there behind him.

Too late. She's seen.

Cassie reaches out a hand and pushes the door open a little

farther. She looks around the room. Flowers—broken, ripped, strange. A few of the plastic-wrapped roses on the fridge give way and slither down to the counter, then slide to the floor.

"Quag, what is this?" Cassie asks. She stands next to him on the landing of the stairs, looking into that kitchen, then looking at him, her brown eyes serious.

"Nothing," says Quag. "It's nothing." He closes the door and runs back down the stairs.

Quag books it out of the apartment building and turns down the alley, ditching Cassie, ditching the mess in the kitchen. Did anyone see his mom hacking down all those flowers? Mrs. Durock? Someone at the library? If those blue flowers are from the library, seems like someone for sure would have seen her. Please don't let them be from the library.

And where is his mom now? What is she doing? How much trouble will she get in this time? How long will this spin last?

He gets to Elizabeth Street by the time the rain starts. Rain swats at his face and hair, and one large drop sneaks down the neck of his T-shirt and slides, cold, down the hollow of his back. He runs across the high school soccer field toward the one dry spot under the overhanging roof of the little booth where they sell burgers and popcorn during games. Big red letters spelling out Snak Shack curl across the metal roof.

Why not Snak Shak? Or Snack Shack? Are we pro-spelling or are we anti-spelling here, people? Can't have it both ways.

He's across the field and sliding down onto the dry strip next to the cinder-block wall before he realizes that Cassie has followed him, that he didn't manage to ditch her at all. She's trotting across the green grass toward him.

Perfect. Way, super, mind-blowingly fabulous. Has she been following him all the way from his house?

He brushes raindrops off his neck and arms as he watches her jog the last bit. She slides down next to him and stretches out her feet in front of her, tapping the sides of her scuffed green sneakers against each other twice. She shivers and shoves her hands into her hoodie pockets.

The ends of her hair are curly, and drops of water hang from the curls. Two fall onto her cheek, merge, and trickle down toward her jawline. Makes Quag want to reach over and brush them off. She drags the sleeve of her sweatshirt across her face, mopping up, and then flips her hood up over her hair and stares off across the grass.

And, normally, this would be literally perfect. Sitting with Cassie. Watching the rain.

But not today. Today Quag doesn't want Cassie here.

He does not want to be the boy Cassie feels sorry for.

What is she seeing as she sits here? Green field, gray rain, scoreboard, mist? A couple of stupid sea gulls who don't know that they're supposed to be out battling the wind and the waves and the briny deep and have ended up on a little soccer field in a town in central New York?

Or is Cassie seeing flowers—broken, ruined, piled? Is she hearing the sound of cellophane on cellophane as the roses slid off the top of the refrigerator?

"What's going on, Quag?" asks Cassie.

He looks out with Cassie at the white lines painted on the green grass, marking off the neat rectangles within rectangles. "Those two birds are super lost, that's what," Quag says, looking at the sea gulls who don't even have the sense to get out of the rain.

"What?" Cassie's looking at him like she is incredibly annoyed with him.

He'll take it. Better than pity.

"Sea gulls," he says, nodding toward the field. "You see any sea?"

"Whatever." Cassie looks off across the green field. Rain slants down, and she pulls her sneakers in farther to keep them dry. "Friends talk to friends about what's going on, Quag," says Cassie.

"Yeah?" says Quag, still looking out into the rain. "Maybe we're not friends."

Even as he says it, he knows it's not true. Cassie is his friend. He's hers. Didn't they plan that whole protest concert together? Didn't she talk to him when all that mess with her dad was going on at the end of the year? Didn't he listen?

But he's never talked to her about his mom. He's never talked to anyone about his mom.

There is a quick movement next to him, and Cassie is on her feet. "If you're going to be a jerk about this, I'm out," she says. She brushes off the back of her jeans and adjusts the hood of her shirt and starts out into the drizzle. When she's a couple of steps away, she turns and shies something at him, sidearm. It hits him in the chest and falls into his lap. Pretzel nibs. Unopened package.

How many of these things does she have anyway?

"Don't be late tomorrow," says Cassie, and she's off across the soccer field, then running up the steps and coming out in the parking lot behind the school. Quag watches her as she crosses the pavement in the rain, crosses the little strip of lawn. He watches her as she runs across the street, turns the corner, and disappears.

She doesn't look back once.

Quag leans his head against the white-painted cinder block, closes his eyes, and listens to the rain. He always thinks that if he just says the right thing to his mom here, or doesn't push her too far when she starts to rev there, that he can stop this. That maybe this time they can stay in that place where she's okay.

Sometimes it seems like it works. For a while. Maybe.

Two weeks ago, she'd been her usual okay-version self—bouncing down next to him on the couch and saying, "Arm-wrestle you for the remote," and then flexing her scrawny arm and acting tough, so that it made Quag laugh, and he'd tossed her the remote without even proving that he could beat her. Hadn't even complained too much when what she decided to watch was some old black-and-white thing with a lot of dancing. Wasn't too bad. If you liked that stuff.

And he'd made her peanut butter toast for dinner, because Quag makes a mean peanut butter toast and because she was so into this old movie, even though anybody in the whole world could have told her what was going to happen after the first five minutes. She'd been lying there on the couch with her red hair spread all over the pillows and this soft look about her as she watched. No way was she going to stop for dinner. And when he brought her the toast, she'd sat up and clapped her hands like he was bringing her a birthday cake or something. She'd closed her eyes and sighed after she took the first bite and said, "You're a good boy, Quag." And they'd watched the rest of the dumb everything-works-out-in-the-end movie while they both ate their toast—thickly spread with extra chunky and with red pepper flakes sprinkled on top. It had been a good night. They'd been okay.

They aren't okay now.

Why can't they stay okay?

BIRDS: SEA GULLS

Maybe soccer-field sea gulls are just sick of eating fish. Maybe they just want their lives to be different. Maybe they're like, "Hey, you feel like a hot dog today?" to their sea gull buddy, and then they fly inland for a game and discover popcorn. And now they have a serious extra-butter-popcorn thing going and are living the dream.

EIGHT

Quag is late the next day, in spite of Cassie's instructions, so he walks in on the middle of a conversation.

"What sort of sicko would vandalize a library?" says Mikey. It feels like the words are acrid, metallic. They leave a taste on Quag's tongue. The air in the room is suddenly too thin.

"Truth," says Jax. "That's just way sad."

"What'd they do?" asks Rhia.

"Trashed the hedge out front, drew this sort of weird, loopy drawing all over the old marble part where you go in the doors. With lipstick or marker or something. Super random. It was on the news last night."

Fabulous. Couldn't be better. This is all Quag needs.

"It's true," says Jax. "They had police tape around that entrance and were trying to clean it off when I went by this morning."

Fabulous. Fabulous. Fabulous.

What Quag feels right now is an overwhelming need to slam out of this room. Or punch someone. But people ask questions when you do stuff like that. So he has to breathe this thin air and pretend to check texts on his phone. He has to be careful not to make eye contact with Cassie.

Cassie's voice is quiet. "Come on, everyone," she says. "Let's get started."

But Mikey's not quite done. "Why would anyone even *do* that?" he says. "I mean, a *library!*"

Quag wishes he hadn't come today. Because Cassie knows too much. Because what if they're not done discussing the library. Because who knows what Cassie is thinking about all this. Because game of the day. Which apparently has not changed since yesterday and which Quag is massively not in the mood for.

Quag's mom didn't come home last night, and though that's happened a few times before, it doesn't happen that often. It freaks Quag out when it does. It's freaking him out today. And that conversation he walked in on isn't helping.

"How about *The Dark Knight Rises?*" says Rhia. "Change one word, and change it from a drama to a comedy."

Mikey is immediately on his feet. "*The Dark Loaf Rises!*" he shouts. "*How Pumpernickel Destroyed the World!*"

Cassie and Rhia laugh.

"*The Snark Knight Rises,*" says Rhia. "High school graffiti artist with wicked sense of humor takes over the school."

Okay. That one is funny. Quag will admit it. But he's still not in the mood for this today.

Where is his mom?

It's not like Quag can't stay by himself. That's not it. He's been staying by himself since he was seven. It's just, where is she?

Okay, technically, Quag knows where she is. He looked up her phone on Track My Phone last night, and she's somewhere up in Syracuse. So maybe at work, but probably not. Moving around too much for that. Maybe still on her all-the-flowers-in-the-world campaign. Maybe on to something else.

Usually, she texts when she's spinning hard enough to not come home. Long, haphazard texts, trailing off into incoherence, true. But something.

"*The Dark Knight Franchises*," offers Cassie. "Bruce Wayne becomes a YouTuber who's all about the ad revenue."

So, what is it that's got him all worked up, then?

Just that he doesn't know if she's okay. That's what.

Is she okay?

"*The Quark Night*, like, not day but night?" Cassie asks the group. "Anything there?"

"Oh!" Mikey is out of his chair again. "*The Quark Night Reprises*! Scientists start a cabaret!"

Jax groans but grins. Cassie smiles. Rhia laughs out loud.

Quag thought about staying home today. Just in case his mom came back. But he knows. When she's revving this hard, she won't be home till she comes down a little.

There's a pause in the game. "Quag?" says Cassie. She looks over at him, questioning. Maybe asking about the game. Maybe also trying to figure out what's going on.

Nope.

"Yeah, okay. I think this one's done," says Cassie.

"I think this one was done at pumpernickel," says Jax. Rhia chucks a pillow at him, but he leans out to catch it and gives her a look. "No pillows near the Beast," he says.

"Right," says Rhia. "My bad."

Everyone acts like the Beast is this big, amazing thing, when it's actually kind of a mess. Quag looks over at it, built on two rolling AV carts that have been zip-tied together. It covers all three shelves of both carts and has more stuff strapped to the sides. Jax is, like always, adjusting something as he stands behind it. The thing doesn't even work right half the time.

Still. Jax's job running the Beast is way better than Quag's I-am-the-Foley-guy gig.

His mom is worse this time. That flower thing. That was way wild. It's usually not that weird when she spins. More out there than other people, for sure, but not all the way to . . . whatever that was.

Here's another thing that bugs Quag about the Beast. It's part soundboard, part portable recording studio, part random crap that doesn't even work yet. Probably never will. But the drama kids treat it like it's some wonder of the world. Whatever. Cassie said the high school was throwing out a bunch of broken stuff, and Jax took everything and fixed it. Borrowed pieces from stuff he couldn't fix.

Doesn't make him a genius. Quag could have figured that out.

But no, Quag is the Foley guy. So instead of working the soundboard, which, even in Beast form, would at least be interesting, Quag is stuck dragging a big, falling-apart cardboard box with "Sound Effects" scrawled on the side in faded orange marker from a closet down the hall. Quag is the Foley guy, so instead of working with Cassie on what the settings should be, Quag is unpacking a rubber chicken, a kid's xylophone, bubble wrap, an umbrella, some gloves, a ring of keys, a zipper that's been ripped out of something, and not two, not three, but four pairs of coconut shells from the box.

Perfect. He'll tell Mikey to work a herd of galloping horses into the script. Mikey's written some old-school detective thing. Should totally fit in.

Nothing about this day is working. Cassie keeps looking over at him like she's trying to figure out what's going on. Mikey just asked him if he was okay. Quag is driving a box full of old shoes and coconut shells instead of some sleek electronic soundboard. And his mom is who knows where, doing who knows what.

What are you supposed to do when your mom chops down all the flowers within five blocks, dumps them on your kitchen floor, and then disappears?

Did not go over that one in health class last year.

Probably "talk to a trusted adult."

Because everybody's been so helpful up to this point. All those people all lined up to help, stretching all the way back to preschool. "If you ever have anything you're worried about, just tell an adult."

But here's the thing. Even if you said, "Hey, in case you haven't bothered to notice this on your own, my mom is out of control," no one really wants to hear that from you. Because it's gonna wreck their Saturday. Now instead of lying around watching the game or heading out in their shiny car to some shiny store to do some shopping for some more shiny, they'll have to try and figure out how to make some pissed-off fourteen-year-old and his out-there mom into somebody else's problem so their whole weekend isn't shot.

So they'll either laugh it off or they'll send you straight to the foster kids people. In the first case, why'd you bother? In the second, now you don't even have an out-there mom. Adults like to think they'll be all kinds of helpful in a case like this, but, honestly, they just don't want to hear it.

Still. The whole thing is freaking him out worse than it usually does. Something seems way more off than usual with this spin. Is she okay? He can imagine a hundred ways she could not be okay. A hundred ways she could be in trouble.

Quag digs through the sound-effects box again. There's a bunch more crap in here, but Quag doesn't care. He throws it all back in and shoves the box into a corner.

Nothing about any of this day is okay.

Rhia has texted, inviting everyone to an afternoon pickup soccer game at Bainbridge Park. Quag doesn't really care about soccer, and he's not in the mood to hear any more commentary about the library, but Cassie is one of the people who texted back that she's in as soon as she gets off her shift at Snarkey's at five. And it is now four minutes till five, and if Quag just happens to be headed up to the soccer game when Cassie gets out . . .

He opens the apartment door and hears a voice in the foyer. Mrs. Durock. Perfect. He does not want to deal with Mrs. Durock.

Mrs. Durock, who is talking loudly to someone about "destruction of property." Perfect, perfect. Couldn't be better.

There's the rumble of a man's voice asking a question.

Who is she talking to? Quag, being sure he sets his feet down on the places on the stair treads that don't creak, makes his way down the first set of stairs to where he can peek around the corner and into the first-floor foyer.

Blue uniforms. A man and a woman. Police.

He pulls his head back to where he can't be seen and flattens himself against the wall. His heartbeat has become something that he can feel in his chest and hear in his ears. He has been so stupid. There's a garbage bag sitting on his kitchen floor, full of moldy flowers. There's dirt spread across the checkered linoleum. There's a stack of dead roses still on the refrigerator.

So stupid.

Will they come up here? Knock on the door? He won't answer. They can't just come in unless they have a warrant or something. At least on TV they can't. But what if they call the landlord? What if the landlord lets them in? Would he let them in?

Do they know about the library?

Quag has been so, so stupid.

He tests each stair as he retreats up the stairwell. When he gets to the door of the apartment, he slowly swings it closed, cringing at the sweep of the rubber weatherstripping along the base of the door, at the clunk of the lock. No one in the world could have missed that heavy thunk.

He pulls a garbage bag from the roll under the sink and sweeps roses off the fridge top, scrambling to pick up the ones that land outside the bag and shoving them inside. He grabs a towel and swishes it through the sink, pushes it across the counters, swirls it across the floor. He should have swept first. This is just smearing everything. Can they hear him doing all this through the floor?

Stupid, stupid, stupid.

When the garbage bag is full, he carries it and the one he filled a couple of days ago through the apartment to his bedroom and carefully slides his window open. No one is in the alley or at the picnic table at Snarkey's. He drags the bags out after him. The biggest heavy one he hides back behind the chimney. The smaller one he wedges between that white pipe that you can sometimes hear the toilet flushing through and some other random pipe.

And then he closes the window and squeezes himself up against the siding where he's almost sure nobody looking out the window or up from the alley can see him. He sits as still as he can, eyes closed, listening to the sound of his own rough-beating heart.

He stays there a long time. Through the shifting of the light across his closed eyelids. Through the sinking of the sun behind the houses. Through the cooling of the evening and some bird telling the whole wide world good night. He sits there until it's dark and quiet, and he can swing down to the fire escape in the night and go along the back ways. He stays out of the slanting rectangles thrown by lit windows and the pools of light under the streetlamps. And he carries the trash bags a few blocks over to where he can toss them into the dumpster behind Clark's Fish Fry.

BIRDS: HIDING

There are birds called nightjars. Really. (Who names these birds?) Nightjars can fly, but they're one of those birds who lay their eggs on the ground again. Seems super weird until you see how good they are at hiding. Quag was watching this video online that was called Spot the Bird, and even though he knew what he was looking for and figured out that whoever made the videos kept putting the bird right in the middle of each frame, he still could not see it at all until they zoomed in way close and drew a white line around it on the screen. Nightjars' camouflage is genius level.

But it has to be. Because the eggs of the kind of nightjar that Quag was watching aren't really camouflaged at all. Like any fool walking by could see the eggs just sitting there looking like lunch. If the nightjar wasn't sitting on them doing their ninja camouflage thing, they'd be goners.

NINE

Today is Mikey's birthday. Which anyone who has been anywhere within fifteen feet of Mikey in the past week should know, because he's told everyone. Every ten minutes.

Cassie comes in carrying a bakery box, and Mikey rockets out of the beanbag. "Is it carrot cake?" he says. "With cream cheese frosting?" When Cassie grins and nods, Mikey goes down on his knees with a squeal and a double-fist pump.

Rhia brings in a big box of Runts for him, and when Mikey opens it, the entire box is all banana-flavored ones, which, okay, are the ones no one likes. Except, apparently, Mikey, who goes into another squeal-fest. Rhia is pretty pleased with herself. "It took me six months of saving the banana ones to get that many," she says. Jax has brought in a "This *IS* Broadway. Where did you *THINK* you were?" T-shirt, probably ordered from extreme-dramanerds.com. Another hit.

So that makes Quag the jerk who didn't bring anything. No one seems to expect him to have brought something, but somehow that makes it worse. Like he's not really part of this.

Fine. Who wants to be part of this? With Mikey sashaying

down the center of the room modeling his stupid T-shirt as Rhia belts out, "There he is, Miss America." Jax slow claps, and Cassie hands him the rubber chicken like it's some sort of bouquet.

Quag goes back to sorting the contents of the stupid Foley-guy sound-effects box. There's a whoopee cushion in there that any other day would seem like a find, but today Quag doesn't even care.

And, no, his mom is not back yet. Thanks for asking.

Rhia is way happy about the whoopee cushion though. She spends the next twenty minutes slipping it onto the chair of anyone who is about to sit down, or sitting on it herself and laughing wildly, until Cassie says, "Oh my gosh! Are you *five*?" and throws it back in the box, even though she's laughing too.

And then everyone gets down to business—Mikey and Rhia reading through the script while Cassie helps them block it for the stage. Jax, who has managed to scrounge yet another microphone from somewhere, is testing whether it picks up sound better than the collection of mics he already has. And Quag? Standing around. Sorting random useless objects. Waiting to add the sound effects.

Perfect.

A few minutes later, Cassie comes by to ask is he okay, he seems tired. But Quag doesn't really feel like talking about it, so he shrugs and lets it drop. He doesn't want to talk to Cassie about this.

Yes, he is tired. Because this week is stretching out to forever. Because nights get filled up with too many thoughts and not enough sleep.

When it's finally time to add the sound effects, Mikey goes all major control freak about exactly how he wants the footsteps to sound and how you have to hear the rain both hitting the umbrella and dripping off the umbrella. So they go over that about sixty-three times while Quag hunches over this blue plastic bin so water won't spill all over the floor. Which it does anyway.

Then Jax wants to try out the new microphone, so they have to do it all again. Cassie and Jax are hovering over the soundboard, heads together, adjusting things. If he were running the soundboard, that would be him working with Cassie.

But Quag is the Foley guy. So instead of standing next to Cassie at the soundboard, he is getting his hands pruney from all this water. Instead of standing next to Cassie at the soundboard, he is folded over this blue tub, dripping water on a striped umbrella. Instead of standing next to Cassie, he is clomping an old pair of black dress shoes across a board. This doing-sound-live idea is the stupidest idea in the universe. This is probably why soundboards were invented—some Foley guy was sick of his T-shirt getting wet every time he splashed a stupid umbrella.

"Come on," says Cassie. "One more time. We've only got fifteen minutes." Fifteen minutes till the big Show Your Stuff session in front of two other groups and Mr. Knudrick.

Can't even wait.

The Beast has been wheeled down the hall. Rhia and Mikey are both wearing gray fedoras, even though it's supposed to be a without-costumes rehearsal today, so why? And Quag, for the second time in a week, drags his stupid box down the hall. Hauls a bin full of water (which keeps sloshing out from under the lid that is supposed to be keeping it in and getting the front of Quag's T-shirt even wetter) up the stairs to the stage. Dumps everything on a table toward the back of the stage where Jax is setting up the mics to pick up every little sound.

Kids from the two groups assigned to give them feedback are coming into the little auditorium and bouncing into their seats, all talking and high-fiving Mr. Knudrick as they arrive.

"Okay, pay attention," says Mikey as he walks past in his fedora. "It'll be dumb if the sounds don't sync up. And it's my birthday, so we don't want it to be dumb."

And that's it.

Quag stands there in his gray T-shirt with the big wet patch on the front, and he hates Mikey Overton. Mikey, who came up with the idea of a radio play. Mikey, who said "Sicko." Quag hates the striped umbrella. He hates the leaky blue bin. He hates Jax and his electrical tape and his stupid Beast. Hates Rhia and Cassie, who are laughing together as they come up the stage steps. He hates the kids in the audience bouncing up and down in their seats and breaking into bits of song from some musical he doesn't know as they wait.

Hates them all.

Fine. They want live sound effects? They'll get live sound effects.

Knudrick is settling everyone down and making an overly cheerful speech. Jax is giving him the thumbs-up to let him know the sound is live. And Quag is reaching deep into his magic Foley box. Because Quag is the Foley guy.

So when Inspector Mikey comes onto the stage, instead of footsteps, there is the sound of coconut-shell horse hooves. Instead of rain falling gently on an umbrella, there's the sound of an unhinged rubber chicken. Jax cuts the sound at this point, but everyone is sitting in the first two rows of the auditorium, and Quag does not need the Beast for this. The kids in the audience are already giggling, and when Mikey leans over to examine a clue, and there is the sound of ripping cloth, they go into full-out laughter. Mikey's red face plays along nicely with the sound effect, which Quag hopes he noticed was perfectly timed. Rhia is trying not to laugh.

And Cassie? Quag is not going to look at Cassie. He's just not. Because he is waiting for Mikey to take Rhia's hand and go down on one knee. And when he does, the glorious and extended sound of a whoopee cushion being skillfully put through its paces spreads through the auditorium.

The crowd goes wild. As they say.

Game of the day, people. How to turn a drama into a comedy in five easy Foley moves.

Mikey, head down and moving at double speed, hurries offstage and clatters down the stairs toward the exit with Rhia close behind. Jax, also heading toward the exit, brushes past Quag, bumping him hard with his shoulder as he goes by and giving him a "Not cool." The door at the bottom of the stairs clangs shut as Mikey, Rhia, and Jax head out into the hall.

And Quag can't really avoid looking at Cassie anymore because she's storming across the stage straight toward him. Cassie is furious. "Are you kidding me, Quag?" she says. "You can be a real jerk sometimes, you know."

"Everybody thought it was funny," says Quag. "You heard all the laughing, right?"

"*Everybody* did not think it was funny," says Cassie, gesturing toward the stage door window at Mikey's retreating figure. "What is your *deal*, Quag?"

Mr. Knudrick comes in from the hall. "Need some help here?" he says to them.

Cassie glares at Quag. "Nope. I've got it," she says to Knudrick.

"Okay," says Knudrick. "But let's talk tomorrow, all right?"

"Sure," says Cassie. She is still laser-eyeing Quag. Quag can feel Knudrick looking at him too, waiting.

Wait all you want, dude.

Knudrick finally takes off across the stage and hops down into the auditorium to talk to another group of kids.

Cassie makes a sound that is equal parts fury and frustration, runs down the stage steps, and slams through the door leading to the hall. Then she's off, trying to catch up with the others, leaving Quag standing by a broken-down cardboard box, holding a whoopee cushion.

AUDIO FILE ON QUAGMIRE TIARELLO'S PHONE

The annoying scraping sound a cardboard Foley box makes when you drag it down the hall.

TEN

"Hey! Tiarello!"

A voice rings out from the baseball dugout in the park as Quag walks past on his way home. Rhia, wearing a Southton Stingers Softball Camp T-shirt and battered black-and-yellow cleats, jogs toward him across the grass. She stops in front of him. "Why were you a jerk to Mikey today?" she says.

What is this? National Protect Mikey Day?

"It was just a joke," says Quag. "I didn't even say anything to Mikey." Quag does not want to hang out in the park discussing with Rhia what he just discussed with Cassie forty minutes ago.

"You don't have to *say* anything," says Rhia. She tosses the softball in her right hand into the mitt on her left. The ball smacks into the pocket with a solid *thwack.* She thwacks it in a couple more times and then takes a step toward Quag, still firing the ball into the mitt.

Seriously?

Quag doesn't back up on principle, but the ball whizzes right past his nose as it lands in the mitt. He shoots Rhia a glare.

"Right now," Rhia says—throw, *thwack,* throw, *thwack*—"I'm kind of being a jerk to you, even though I'm not saying anything mean." She thwacks the ball into the mitt one more time and then reaches out with one of her huge hands and palms Quag's head. Quag shakes off her hand and scowls at her. She grins. "And now I'm being a total jerk to you, because I'm reminding you that I'm five eleven, and stronger than you, and can run faster than you ever dreamed of running. So I could pretty much keep that hand on your head if I wanted to." Rhia tucks the mitt and ball under her arm. "You don't have to say anything to be a jerk."

There is a flurry of movement over by the dugout as a runner comes in from third but is thrown out before she crosses the plate. "Next time, Leeza!" Rhia yells across at her, clapping her hands. "Next time! No worries!"

She turns back to Quag, and her face gets serious again. "Cassie and Jax and Mikey and me have worked together at ArtCamp off and on for, like, years," says Rhia. "We're a team."

Another flurry from the dugout. Heads pop out from around the side. Cries of "Rhia! You're up!"

Rhia nods toward the field. "Gotta go save the world, Tiarello. But don't be a jerk again, 'kay?"

She jogs back toward the dugout, tossing her mitt to one teammate and catching the long black bat another throws to her. She kisses the handle of the bat and walks out to the plate.

And because Quag is mad at her for that hand-on-the-head crap, he hopes she'll choke, hopes she strikes out, that she has to walk back to the dugout a little smaller. But part of him is not surprised when she steps into a pitch, lifts it cleanly over the infield, and rips it into a seam between the outfielders. Part of him can't help watching her run. She runs like you would imagine someone would run if they planned on saving the world. Part of him is not surprised at all when she doesn't even hesitate at second, though the outfielders have gotten themselves sorted out by then. And when she makes it safe to third by sliding hard and fast under the tag, all he feels is respect. Because Quagmire Tiarello is someone who understands what nerve looks like and gives credit where it's due.

But when all of Rhia's dugout goes delirious with wild, chanting joy, and when Rhia pops to her feet and says something to the third baseman that makes both Rhia and her start laughing together like they have both just found a new best friend, Quag feels a billowing surge of black jealousy whirl up. It makes it hard to breathe, so he turns away and heads down the path without looking back. Stupid Rhia.

And stupid Mikey.

It pisses Quag off that he is actually crunching down a path in Bainbridge Park feeling jealous of Mikey Overton. Overexcited, let's-play-a-game Mikey. Because Mikey has people who go snarly if someone even thinks too loud about being mean to him. Because everyone knows to bring Mikey the banana pieces out of a package of Runts. Because they all know Mikey wants a carrot cake on his stupid birthday. And bring him one.

It's not like Quag is some loner loser who doesn't have friends. He does. Kids who sit at the same lunch table at school with him.

But Quag knows his friends keep their distance when they think he's going too far in mixing it up with a teacher. Even if the teacher deserves it. Even if they secretly wish they had the guts to call that teacher out themselves. And Quag knows that he doesn't get invited over to his friends' houses. Nobody from Quag's lunch table is going to bring him a carrot cake on his birthday.

Fine by him. Who would even want a stinking carrot cake? Only old ladies. And stupid Mikey Overton. Nobody at the lunch table even knows when Quag's birthday is, anyway. He'd kind of dropped the habit of telling people once he got to middle school.

Quag remembers elementary school with the birthday poster in Ms. Santana's class, and the birthday chair in Ms. Tyler's class, and that stupid birthday crown with streamers in Ms. Abaye's class. And Quag would never admit this to anyone, but his elementary school dream had been to have his mom bring cupcakes in on his birthday. Which, okay, that makes him totally sound like some loser kid in a make-them-cry commercial, but, hey, it was what he had wanted. To have it be his birthday and have his mom appear at the classroom door and push it open, holding it with a foot and pivoting gracefully through like Aliyah Mitchell's mom did, hands full of huge silver plates piled with those sugar-cocaine-frosting birthday cupcakes that you had to special order from the cafeteria two weeks in advance so that they'd be guaranteed allergy-free for everyone.

By fourth grade you had to start saying, "Who wants some nasty cupcakes made by hairnet ladies?" when the kids asked you if your mom was coming. But really, nobody was buying it. Everybody wants to be the kid whose mom brings the birthday cupcakes.

His mom's still not home when he gets there, and now this whole thing is really messing with his head. She almost never stays out more than a day or two. He texts again, calls again. Going straight to voicemail. So is her phone dead?

He bonks around the apartment for a while. Watches the dumpster cam, but it seems stupid now. He has to get out of the house. Anything but the waiting. Even hanging out with the duck is better than the waiting. Quag heads down toward the lake. But when he comes up on the street that leads to Cassie's house, Quag's feet turn left at that corner instead of the right that would take him down to the lake.

So this is a horrible idea.

Cassie definitely does not want to see him right now. And as he comes down the street, he can see Cassie sitting on her front porch. Looking his way. Now he can't even bail.

When he gets to her house, something turns him up her front walk. Even though he knows she's still way mad at him. Even though she'll send him packing. Because Cassie doesn't take crap from anyone.

And she doesn't exactly open her arms wide when she sees him. Just, steely-eyed, watches as he walks toward her. The sidewalk stretches out longer and longer under his feet, and at the same time, somehow he gets there faster than he's ready to with her looking at him like that.

"Coming to say you're sorry?" Cassie asks. Which just makes him mad all over again. Because, no. He is not coming to say he's sorry.

Why does he even bother? This whole thing is messed up. Cassie thinks he's a jerk. Jax is pissed. Mikey's all hurt. Rhia has put him on notice. And maybe he was kind of a jerk today, but whatever. He isn't going to crawl. Beg for forgiveness.

A red car pulls up in front of Cassie's house, and a woman with dark hair hits the horn twice and then calls to them from the open window. "Groceries!" she yells.

"Come on," says Cassie, hopping up from the porch. "It's Aunt Becca." Like this should mean something to Quag. Like because it's Aunt Becca, he should be up for doing whatever she needs done with these groceries, no questions asked.

But here he is, following Cassie down the front walk and letting some Aunt Becca lady, who he doesn't even know, load him up with four bags. Nodding when she says, "Black one has ice cream, so put it straight in the freezer, okay?" Like he just hangs out on random front sidewalks waiting to put random ice cream into random freezers in houses he's never been in. He probably looks like a loser, shuffling along the sidewalk dragging these bags that have cartoon penguins and hippos and dancing giraffes on them.

But part of him is thinking, at least he'll see where Cassie lives. He really wants to see where Cassie lives.

He props open the screen door with his foot while he drags all the lions and tigers and penguins inside and comes around the corner into a small, bright kitchen that smells like stew cooking. Which you wouldn't think would smell good in July, but it way does. He finds the refrigerator and puts like six cartons of ice cream in, and all of them are good flavors. Plus, there are three boxes of those big ice-cream bars covered in thick chocolate.

Then he stands there while this Aunt Becca lady hands him cans of tomatoes and tells him which cupboard they go in and tosses him bunches of green leafy stuff and tells him which part of the refrigerator those go in. He stands there while she hands him and Cassie each one of those massive ice-cream bars. And when Aunt Becca bites into hers and the chocolate shrapnels off onto the counter and floor, and she sighs and says, "So dangerous and so good," he realizes that he's smiling a little. And that when he looks over at Cassie, maybe Cassie is thinking about smiling a little.

Maybe.

He can tell Cassie is still mad at him, but the ice cream is sweet and cold, and somehow it's enough for right now. To just stand in the same kitchen with Cassie eating something this good and her aunt not seeming like she wants to get rid of him. Or even that she just invited him in so she could keep an eye on him. Just everybody eating ice cream together, like they've known each other for a long time and will know each other for a long time after this.

Quag feels the sun spilling in through the bank of windows behind him shining warm on his shoulders and smells the stew in the Crock-Pot on the counter and listens to Aunt Becca telling Cassie about someone at the grocery store who told her to tell Cassie hi. And it feels okay. Even with the worry of his mom missing still pinging around in the top left corner of his brain, it feels okay. So when this Aunt Becca turns to him and says, "You must be Quag," it doesn't seem as weird as adults saying stuff like that usually does. He almost isn't surprised when she says, "Want to stay for lunch?"

And Cassie looks at Aunt Becca and then looks at Quag and shrugs. Gives a quick quirk to one side of her mouth. Almost a smile. Definitely. Like maybe she wouldn't mind if he stayed.

Quag almost says yes.

He almost does. But he knows that he'll have to fake a text to his mom and an answer. He knows he'll have to lie when this Aunt Becca birder person asks him questions. About birds. Which she definitely knows more about than he does; there are photographs she's taken all along the hall that are cool enough that he kind of wanted to stop and look them over if no one had been watching, and most of them were of birds he doesn't even know the names of. So questions from this photographer/birder aunt of Cassie's are out.

Worse, Quag is noticing that he is developing a problem with saying no to Cassie. It bugs him. So he says no now. Even though the stew smells good. Even though this Aunt Becca person seems okay. Even though Cassie almost smiled. He just does it to prove to himself that he can still do it. And because somehow it hurts to be here, where everything is warm and right, while his mom is lost.

"Don't be late tomorrow," Cassie says to him as he heads toward the door. She is not smiling now. She is not giving him anything. She's just watching him leave.

He walks to the lake and watches the light on the water. He walks home, eats some cereal, and scans the footage from the dumpster cam. Waits for his mom to come home.

AUDIO FILE ON QUAGMIRE TIARELLO'S PHONE

The sound of the lake rolling the pebbles along the shore.

ELEVEN

Quag is late. A little.

Because sleeping last night was not a thing. He kept waking up thinking he heard his mom. But then it wasn't. Just some high school kids making noise. Just Durock yelling at them. Just a car driving by. But not his mom's car, not the blue car his mom calls Rosie. Just fifty other things that weren't her.

When Quag wakes up the next morning after all that not-quite-sleeping, there's just time to throw on a cleanish shirt and shorts and get himself up to the Y, a little late.

Doesn't improve his mood at all when he opens the door of the room to see Jax and Rhia and Cassie and Mikey with four chairs pulled up in a circle that leaves no room for a fifth chair. Cassie looks at him exactly how she looked at him yesterday, not giving him anything.

"Quag, can you wait outside for a minute?" she says.

Nope. Not while you all vote me off the island. He should have seen this coming. Not happening. He'll vote himself off if he's leaving.

Quag turns to go.

"No, wait," says Mikey, twisting around in his chair. "Wait! Wait! I think we're good." He points at Rhia. "You're good with it, right?"

Rhia leans back in her chair. "I'm okay with it."

"Jax?" says Mikey.

Jax interlaces his long fingers. "I don't love it. But I'll do it, if it's what you really want."

"It is!" says Mikey. "It's gonna be awesome! Cassie?"

"He shouldn't have done it the way that he did it." Her arms are folded tight across her chest.

"Yeah, yeah," says Mikey, waving away the comment with his hand. "Agreed. But it's gonna be awesome! Right?"

Cassie shrugs.

"Right!" says Mikey, turning his chair toward Quag with a scrape. "We want to do it with the mismatched sound effects," he announces.

"What?" says Quag.

"The radio play!" says Mikey. "I was telling my sister about what happened yesterday, and we were both super mad. Like she was seriously ready to come chase you down and, I don't even know, do damage. But then all of the sudden, I started kind of laughing, and I was like, 'Okay, but it was a little funny, though.' And she was like, 'It so was not, Mikey!' but then she started laughing too, and she was like, 'A whoopee cushion, Mikey? Really? Super lowbrow.' But the thing is, it *was* funny. People were laughing. A lot. So anyway, we want to do the radio play like it's written, but play it off against comic sound effects. Even better ones. Because it will be genius!"

What is wrong with Mikey? You diss him in front of an auditorium full of kids, and by the next morning he's all, "Let's do it again"?

Everyone is looking at Quag like they're expecting an answer from him. Mikey, all excited, because something is seriously wrong with Mikey. Jax in the opposite camp—a look on his face that clearly says, "Yeah, we are not friends, and I do not trust you, and if you mess up again, we'll have trouble." Which, okay, Quag can at least respect that. Rhia, kind of amused by the whole thing and willing to make peace. And Cassie.

Quag's not sure what to make of Cassie. Because Cassie's just sitting there with her arms folded tight. And the look that she has on her face . . . Quag doesn't know. He wants to look at her long enough to figure out what that look means, but he doesn't want everyone watching him. He wishes she was still just furious at him, maybe. Maybe she is.

Once, Quag saw this little kid at a playground. The kid's older brother had just made fun of him in front of his older friends. And the kid had stood there at the edge of the playground, arms folded tight around himself, face hard like he was concentrating on . . . what? Revenge? No, that wasn't it. More like his brother was someone he had never seen before, someone that he had to understand within the next ten minutes. More like maybe his arms were wrapped around himself to keep him from flying apart. He hadn't taken his eyes off his brother the whole time Quag watched him.

That's how Cassie is looking at him. Maybe. From what he could see in the seconds he dared look. Like she doesn't know who he is. Which makes Quag feel like his skin is too tight, and he wants to crawl out of it.

But there are three other pairs of eyes looking at him, and Mikey is saying, "So will you?" And all Quag can manage is a shrug. Which, of course, Mikey takes as agreement and sends up a cheer. And then Rhia is pulling up another chair, and Jax is getting out a pen and the ratty blue notebook he carries around, and everyone is talking about sound effects.

Everyone except Cassie, who is quiet. Everyone except Quag, who just wants Cassie to look at him. To smile, to scowl, to throw a left hook, he doesn't care. He can see her across from him, picking at the threads of her ripped jeans, turning her head to follow the conversation as it bounces between Jax and Rhia and Mikey, but pretty obviously avoiding the Quag section of the room.

Quag throws out the suggestion "hyenas" to one of Rhia's questions, just to test whether Cassie will look at him. She doesn't. But for a second, there is a tiny quirk to her lips that would have turned into a smile if she'd let it.

He'll wear her down, then.

A few minutes later, when Quag says, "We really need to use sound files for some of this stuff," Cassie does turn toward him.

"That's not what Mikey wants, Quag," she says, looking at Quag like he'd suggested they eat someone's pet cat.

"I don't really care about doing all the sounds live anymore," says Mikey, leaning over to look at the list in Jax's notebook. "I just want it to be hilarious. I want people dying in the aisles. I mean hyenas are going to be kind of hard to do live. Blue whales too."

But Cassie is still laser-eyeing Quag. "I'm sure Quag can do a hyena impression," she says. "And a blue whale." Her voice is sharp, unfriendly. It feels like a challenge. The room goes quiet.

Quag looks at her, and he lets all that fierce, all that unfriendly, all that challenge, all that—is there hurt in those eyes?—he lets all of it in. He doesn't blink. He doesn't look away.

And then he takes a chance.

He flashes Cassie a big smile and lets out the low A-OOOOOOO-GAAAAA of a blue whale. Quag stretches out that whale song as Cassie's eyes go wide and wider and as the other kids dissolve into laughter. And when Quag pulls his arms into his sides and tops the whole thing off with a couple of fin flaps— which, to be fair, is more of a dolphin thing, but whatever—what happens on Cassie's face is like the sun rising over the lake, like that second when you've waited and waited, sitting up on the roof outside your room as the dawn slides up the other side of the world, and then there's that second when it spills over and light slides across the water, and it's the most beautiful thing you've ever seen.

That's what happens on Cassie's face as the surprise in those brown eyes sweeps away the fierceness and spills over into a smile that brushes across her face and breaks out into a laugh. It feels good to have done that to that face.

And when Cassie comes up from her laugh and says, "Quag,

you are such a dork," somehow that feels even better. Because it means she has forgiven him, maybe. Or will.

After that, it goes easier, and they come up with a good plan. New scenes, new sounds. Quag and Jax are over at the Beast trying to download a file of a hyena and something that will approximate a spaceship engine. They're practicing some live stuff too. They're going to do both. They're doing the blue whale live. The whole thing is pretty funny. It might be amazing. Cassie looks over at Quag from where she's helping Rhia and Mikey with a new scene and kind of shakes her head and smiles.

And Quag smiles back.

AUDIO FILE ON QUAGMIRE TIARELLO'S PHONE

Jax and Mikey and Rhia giggling so hard that Mikey and Rhia can't say their lines, and Jax can hardly breathe.

TWELVE

They finish the script before the end of the day. They find the files. They run through the first bit, and even Jax breaks into this high-pitched helpless giggle as they go. That sets Rhia off, which sets Mikey off, which makes Cassie put a hand over her mouth, which makes Quag grin. When they run out of time, they all walk together down the hall toward the big doors leading out of the Y, everyone laughing and throwing out ideas about ways they could work a platypus into the mix. Spaceships filled with platypuses. Platypuses reading the parking meters. Honestly, it's pretty funny when everyone's on a roll like this. It feels good.

And when Cassie says, "I'm sure Quag could do a beautiful platypus impression," then smiles up at him and bumps her shoulder against his arm while they're walking together, it's like something in Quag jumps and then doesn't come back down. Because it feels like something new, something that hasn't happened before. Something he wants to happen again. So he bumps her back, but gently, gently, and then he keeps floating along beside her down the hall.

They join a big bunch of kids heading out the doors, and Quag has a second, two seconds, three seconds, as they're walking out to see that the sky is blue and the leaves are green and the world is beautiful. And then they all step into that world, and the door shuts behind them, and they all turn together toward a sound.

And the beautiful is gone.

Quag learned long ago not to mix home and school. Not any time he could help it. Because sometimes his mom was the fun mom on the field trip bus, the mom everyone liked. But other times it was like watching a pile of oil-soaked rags smolder in the corner, wondering whether you could keep things at the slow-burn level or whether this time they'd flare up, and flames would start licking up the wall. At worst, the fire came bursting through the door and roaring across everyone and everything. And that's what's happening now.

His mom is pulled up in front of the Y, car parked halfway up on the sidewalk, hanging out the window and yelling Quag's name over and over while also hitting the horn.

Subtle.

The kids coming out the door of the Y are looking at her. The people walking their dogs on the path next to the Y are looking at her. Rhia, Mikey, Jax, and Cassie are all looking at her. Everyone within five hundred feet is looking at her. She's pretty hard to miss.

Cassie lays her fingertips on Quag's arm. "Quag, you okay?" she asks.

"Yeah," says Quag. "I gotta go."

But Cassie doesn't let go of his arm. "Pick up five glazed

doughnuts for the group tomorrow, okay?" She presses a crumpled twenty-dollar bill into his palm. "From Benny's. It's right on your way."

"Right. Five glazed." Quag shoves the twenty into his pocket. He needs to get in the car.

"Don't be late," Cassie says.

Why does she always say that?

The horn is continuous now, a never-ending blare. He has to get in the car. He has to get this whole mess out of here. Back to the apartment. Hidden.

Quag turns toward Cassie in what he hopes reads as a nonchalant way. "No problem. I'll be sitting on the steps tomorrow morning waiting for you," he says.

They do not make it back to the apartment. Because they're driving to Buffalo to get a hot dog. Not just any hot dog, according to his mom. An extra-charred dog with all the works from Ted's, wherever that is. They are driving to Buffalo to get a hot dog, even though Quag has pointed out that he is pretty good at charring hot dogs right on top of the stove burner at home, and Buffalo is like three hours away, and who cares about Ted's.

The car skims down the highway, and his mom is talking, talking, but Quag's not in the mood to listen. It's hot, and Rosie's AC is a joke, so Quag rolls down a window and lets the hot air blow over him and thinks about what he should do. Get her back home. Obviously. But that suggestion is not going anywhere until he can get her past this Ted's thing. Or on to something else.

Sometimes it's just better to go with it for a while. Drive to stinking Buffalo, get the stupid hot dog, steer her to that something else. Like maybe a search for the best shakes in upstate, and then after they've hit a couple places, suggest they have to compare those shakes against Foster's. Wind her home that way.

If he can just get her home.

Get her to sleep. Yeah. That's probably not happening.

But at least get her up to the apartment.

If he can get her home.

They order the extra-charred dogs with everything. They order the half-and-half, which turns out to be a greasy twist of paper full of half onion rings and half fries. Whoever invented that combo is a genius. They order loganberry shakes, which are good, and loganberry juice, which is nasty. Kind of reminds Quag of when he was little and used to eat Kool-Aid powder straight out of the jar in the cupboard. And Quag is eating—salty hot dog, sweet shake, greasy rings. But now that she's ordered, his mom is on to her own something else.

She's taking selfies with groups of strangers in front of this creepy fiberglass sculpture of a hot dog that has a face and a chef's hat. She is talking to everyone—to people in the booths and to a guy coming out of the bathroom. To a little kid who runs and hides behind his big sister while Quag's mom laughs too loud and says, "Oh, he's shy! You don't have to be shy, honey!"

And it's too much. You can see it. Because first the people were smiling and laughing with her, and they'd crowded in for selfies, but now they're turning their faces away. And she's not seeing it.

But Quag is seeing it. They need to get out of here.

Quickly, he gathers up her untouched loaded hot dog, her half-melted shake, her juice, and slides the whole mess into the trash. She almost never eats when she's like this.

He picks up her big yellow purse from the bench. Thing is like a freaking suitcase. He stashes her twist of fries in it. Picks up his own shake. Goes after his mom.

Too late.

Because his mom has somehow gotten into something with the father of a family at a booth halfway across the room, and he's saying, "Back off, lady," and she's laughing and saying, "Wow. A little uptight, are we?" And now the talk around the room is stopping, and the heads are turning—the cute girl with a ponytail who put the toppings on their hot dogs, the kid with the hairy arms who's running the grill, an old guy and his wife who came in holding hands.

The big dude is standing chest out in front of his mom. The woman behind him is reaching to put a hand on his back while gathering their little girl up against her side.

They need to get out of here.

Quag walks up behind his mom, nodding to the guy who's upset so he'll know they're on the same side, and wraps his long arm around his mom's bony shoulders, tightening his grip just enough so that when he walks, he takes her with him as he goes. It's easier than it used to be, now that he's bigger than she is. But she still throws an elbow into his ribs and tries to shrug him off, making a little of his shake splash out. It leaves four crooked, pale purple spots on the shiny red floor.

Quag tightens his grip around her shoulders and walks her toward the door. The old guy who has been sitting with his wife at a table near the front gets up and opens the door to let them through. They need to get in the car. They need to get gone.

She's yelling at him by the time he steers her to the car. She's yelling back at the guy in the shop. She's yelling at the people in the lot. Quag sets the shake down on the roof so he can keep a hold of her wrist while digging around with his one free hand in the stupid purse. Where are the keys?

He finally finds them and gets the door unlocked and half pushes, half hips her into the car. She arches her back against the seat and slams both palms down on the horn. He can see a row of faces inside Ted's watching. Then he's around the other side and into his seat. He jams the keys into the ignition. "Mom," he says. "Let's go home."

She starts the car up, but she's not happy about it. "Fine," she says. "We'll go home, and then we can sit around home doing absolutely nothing. Happy?" They screech out of the parking lot and onto the street out front. Quag glances out the back window and sees a long stripe of purple on Rosie's glass. He left his shake on the roof.

He leans his head against the window and closes his eyes. He's tired. This week has gone on too long. But at least they're headed home.

AUDIO FILE ON QUAGMIRE TIARELLO'S PHONE

Tires on pavement.

THIRTEEN

Quag wakes with his face crushed against the car window. It's dark.

It shouldn't be dark.

"Where are we?" he asks.

"How should I know?" snaps his mom. So she's still mad.

Quag finds his phone in the cupholder and thumbs to maps. The pulsing dot that is them is sliding along a yellow road in a pale green Ohio. Sliding west.

He is suddenly, shatteringly awake.

They should not be moving west. Home is east.

They should not be in Ohio.

It should not be dark.

What time is it? He pops out of maps, and it is 4:37 a.m. He is pulsing along near Sandusky, Ohio. On some thin bridge over dark water in Ohio, and his mind is tracing back across the map, over what must have happened while he slept, back past towns called Mentor and Conneaut and Erie and Ripley—all the wrong way—so that now it is 4:37 a.m., and he is in Sandusky, Ohio.

Why are they in Sandusky, Ohio?

He's doing the math in his head, but the map says six hours and twenty-three minutes to Southton Falls, and he already knows. He knows. So he is pounding on the roof of the car with his fist. There is no way they can make it. Even if they turned around right now, even if they had turned around two hours ago, there is no way that he is going to "no problem" be at the Y, sitting on the steps, waiting for Cassie.

His mom is yelling at him to knock it off and smacking at his chest with the hand not on the steering wheel, but he doesn't knock it off, and he doesn't care, because there is no way. He can feel this sweet new thing with Cassie stretching back along that stinking yellow road in pale green Ohio, pulling tighter and tighter until he's not waiting on the steps under the ArtCamp sign, and he's not walking down the halls with Mikey and Jax and Rhia. And he can see Cassie get that hard look on her face, realizing. He's not coming.

Because he screwed up. He believed his mom when she said they'd be home in three hours. He fell asleep. He ended up over dark water in Ohio.

That thing he had with Cassie stretches out along all those roads back through Ohio, Pennsylvania, New York, and it is pulled too tight. It will snap. It will snap. And none of the things he hadn't even let himself hope for will happen, because his mom is a liar, liar, liar. So he's yelling and punching the roof of her old car, but none of that is going to fix anything. It's six hours and twenty-three minutes back to Southton Falls.

Everything is broken.

. . .

The first text from Cassie comes in at 8:11.

> Where are you?

Because he sure isn't sitting on the stairs waiting, is he? He can't even get his mom to turn the car around. They argued about it until his mom got even more revved up than she had been after Ted's, and Quag had to drop it for a while.

At 8:17, two more texts.

> Are you getting the doughnuts?
>
> Get over here, we have to show Mr. K what we're doing in like ten minutes.

Then a call. Which he doesn't answer.

Because what is there to say? I'm in the middle of Ohio, and I don't know why, or where I'm going, or when I'll be back?

Perfect.

The wheels go around, and the sun shines down, and the tires thrum against the ribbon of a road. And where are they? And does it matter? Does it matter that the stinking sign says mile forty-three? Forty-three from what? Forty-three to where?

At mile fifty-seven, Cassie starts texting again:

> **Are you kidding me?**

Mile sixty-one:

> **Where were you?**

Mile eighty-four:

> **What is going on, Quag? Consider telling the truth because I'm pissed enough at you without you lying to me.**

How do you start telling the truth?

The wheels go around, and the rain comes down, and the tires hiss against the road. And it might seem like they are driving in a straight line, like they're headed somewhere, but they're not. They're riding that same wild circle they always ride, and his mom, spinning, is the center of that circle. She will spin and spin, until they spin too fast, and every stinking thing will come apart—a tire rolling off across the grass, windshield wipers breaking away and flying, still swiping at the air as they sail past. Fenders, steering wheel, muffler tumbling by. The house they lived in during second grade, that friend he almost made in kindergarten, a soundboard from a concert he was part of in eighth grade, Cassie. Cassie, hair rumpling in the fierce wind of this spin, hand reaching out like Quag could catch her if he tried.

But he knows he can't.

Three texts come in. All stacked up along the left margin of his phone.

> Are
> You
> Alive?

Quag slides his thumb across the glass and gives the question a thumbs-up. Then he shuts down his phone, leans against the window, and watches the gray world go by.

BIRDS: NAVIGATION

Birds have these mad skills for finding their way around when they're going somewhere. Scientists are like, "Whoa, how do they even do that?" They think maybe birds can actually see the magnetic fields of the earth as they fly. They're not even quite sure how. Some people think they're using quantum physics and these things called cryptochromes in the birds' eyes. Like the light from a star hits the cryptochromes, and it makes something called a radical pair happen, and then, because the radical pairs are linked and can always tell where they are in relation to each other and to the earth's magnetic field, the bird always knows where it is in the world. Something like that. Anyway, some little bird can fly all across the world, but birds always know where they're going.

They're never just going who knows where, who knows why.

FOURTEEN

Quag is checking where they are on his phone when it buzzes. It's a text from the drama kids group chat. Mikey wants to know what word would change some random movie from a tragedy to a comedy.

But, actually. Sometimes there's just not any one word that will do that.

FIFTEEN

Quag has had dreams before where he had extra arms, but it didn't seem like a big deal—just meant he could carry a gym bag, drink from his water bottle, punch a number into his phone, and unlock a door all at the same time. He has had dreams where when he stepped on the sidewalk leading to his apartment, it cracked under his feet, the fissures spreading out from each step like he was walking on thin, gray ice. Quag has had dreams where he could fly as long as he was holding a bag of onion rings. But Quag has never had a dream where he woke up with a crick in his neck from sleeping against a car window. The neck crick is what clues him in that this is the real deal. Because the view from the car window could be something from a dream. It could.

He sees a squat cinder-block building painted a shade of hot pink that nothing on earth should be painted. On the roof of that eyeball-searing pink cube sits an old green car with massive chrome bumpers and tail fins you could cut yourself on. Just in case someone, somehow, has missed the fact that "Hello, there is a car on the roof," a giant arrow with lights chasing around and around and around announces "Falling Car Café."

So, that's a good idea. Let's put a hunk of steel on some sketchy-looking old roof until the car, which the sign has clearly stated is in the act of falling, finishes that tumble and mashes some guy inside trying to eat a plate of toast and eggs.

But, apparently, this is a real car, and a real sign, and a real café in the real world, because Quag can't fly, has no onion rings, and he has a crick in his neck that feels seriously reality-based. Also, the driver's seat in his own non-tail-finned non-flying car sitting right here on the ground is empty.

The empty driver's seat wakes Quag up in a hurry. Perfect. Couldn't be better. He is who knows where, and his mom has gone missing again. How long has he been asleep? How long has she been gone?

He sits up fast. There's his mom, walking quick across a pot-holed parking lot with her yellow purse under her arm, and (what the heck?) she's climbing up on the running board of some shiny, black, wide-hipped pickup truck and grabbing something out of the truck bed. Then she's off across the lot. Quag spins around in his seat and checks if anyone saw her, and then he's out of the car and after her as fast as he can go without making someone wonder what's up.

But at this point, she's already headed into the building. By the time Quag gets to the door, he can see her through the glass, walking to the back of the room, pitching her giant bag into a booth, and continuing on through a door marked "Ladies."

Perfect. Let's do another restaurant. That went so well last time.

Quag hauls open the door of the café, setting off a couple of cowbells hung above it. The room is all done up in this "used to be cute" diner style—the black-and-white-checkered floors now with edges of tiles peeled up here and there, and a dingy gray trail worn through where too many people have walked, the red vinyl booths patched with silver duct tape. Square, sunburned men in ball caps sit at the counter, digging into plates of scrambled eggs or downing cups of coffee.

Quag slides into the booth where his mom's purse is and digs out her wallet. There's a hefty orange-handled wrench in the purse. (Is that what she just took from the pickup?) How much money do they have left? Only three lousy bucks in the bills department. He scoots the caddy holding the ketchup and Cholula over, so the sharp-eyed waitress behind the counter can't see, and counts the change from the coin purse behind it—$2.73 in dimes, nickels, and pennies. Great. Quag takes the debit card out of his mom's wallet and pockets it, along with the dollar bills.

Even if the sign behind the waitress didn't scream "CASH ONLY" in big red letters, they can't use the card. They've only got 121 bucks in the bank, and they're going to get stuck out here (wherever here is) with not enough money to get home.

He has got to get his mom to turn around. How can he get his mom to turn around? None of the usual stuff is working this time.

"What can I get you?" The solid, all-business waitress, thin brown hair pulled back into a ponytail at the nape of her neck, has appeared. Quag covers the little pile of coins with his hand. He wishes he'd had a little more time to look over the menu painted on the wall behind the counter, but with $5.73 max to spend, it probably doesn't matter. The waitress, whose name tag says she is "JoAnna, your helpful server," waits, pen over her order pad.

"Two small coffees," says Quag.

The order pad goes back in the pocket, unwritten on.

"Here or to go?"

"To go."

"Got it," says JoAnna. She turns and makes her way back behind the counter and from there through the swinging door to the kitchen. A gust of bacon-scented air whooshes back into the diner with the swinging of the door.

Quag hauls out his phone to figure out where they are. The battery is getting low, and there's no charger that fits his phone in the car. But they're in Iowa, apparently. Right. Couldn't be better. Because if you keep driving west, always west, west, west for enough hours, you are going to end up in Iowa. And here is what Quag wants to know: Are they going to drive west until they drive off some beach in California and the ocean closes over Rosie's roof? Because this west thing is getting them farther and farther from where he wants to be and closer and closer to not having enough money to get back home. Then what?

Quag picks at the peeling wood veneer on the napkin holder. He feels for Cassie's twenty still rolled tight in his front pocket. He'll have to spend it. Since Ted's, he's only had the leftover fries and rings from his mom's purse and half a stale granola bar that he found in the back seat. A coffee is not going to do much. He shoves the rolled twenty farther down in his pocket.

Not yet.

He closes his eyes and leans back against the booth, tipping his head to try to stretch out the knot in his neck. He should never have gotten in the car. She wouldn't have gone if he'd refused to get in the car. Would she? But now what's he supposed to do? Tell the guy at the counter that he's been kidnapped by his own mom, who is not okay right now and refuses to go home?

Not really an option.

A huge plate is clattered down on the table in front of Quag by the no-nonsense JoAnna. It's so big, it's more like a platter. It's filled with food.

"This isn't mine," says Quag. "I ordered two coffees."

"Thursday special," JoAnna says briskly. "Every fourth customer on Thursdays gets the Full Meal Deal on the house. Lucky you, kid. You're a fourth. It's Thursday. No charge."

Quag gives her a long sideways look.

JoAnna, your helpful server, gives it right back to him, no smile, all business, as she shuttles a few more dishes from her arms to his table. She pours out the two coffees Quag ordered into thick white cups with chipped saucers. Her hands are blunt-fingered, efficient. "Look, kid," she says, finishing up. "You got a problem with my cooking?"

"No," says Quag.

"Glad to hear it," says JoAnna, turning from the table. "Eat up."

She heads off toward a group of old guys wearing VA hats coming in the front door.

Quag looks down at the table. A waffle that covers most of the plate. Butter melted into all the squares and warm syrup mixed with the butter. Big chunks of scrambled eggs, speckled with pepper, steam rising from them. Eight thick slices of bacon cooked so they're all the way crispy. Hash browns so hot they're still fizzing. Applesauce in a bowl with a little cinnamon sprinkled across it. Orange juice in a glass so tiny it seems like a toy or something.

The orange juice has floaty bits in it, and usually Quag doesn't like that stuff in his orange juice, but today it tastes really good. Everything tastes really good—the spongy heaviness of the syrup-soaked waffle, the salt and grease of the bacon sharp on his tongue. Everything. Even the applesauce doesn't taste like regular applesauce somehow.

His mom finally comes out of the bathroom—tense, wound up, saying why'd you order all that, we need to get going. She takes a slice of bacon but waves the rest off and drinks her coffee quick, saying hurry up, hurry up.

But Quag does not hurry up. He chews and swallows and chews and swallows and wonders why butter and syrup melted together are way more than twice as good as either one by itself. He eats the eggs while they are still so hot they almost burn. He wipes up the last of the syrup with his finger and a bit of hash brown.

When they leave, Quag takes one of the dollar bills he'd fished out of his mom's wallet and scoots the stack of coins from behind the ketchup holder to add to it. He hopes JoAnna will know that he's sorry that it's mostly change and that there isn't much of it.

He thinks she'll know. He's watched the other customers come and go as he ate. And although at least nine people ordered while he finished off that waffle, that orange juice, that bacon, no one else got the Thursday special.

AUDIO FILE ON QUAGMIRE TIARELLO'S PHONE

The clinking of silverware, cowbells over a door.

SIXTEEN

They're driving too fast.

Maybe there are cars that can go this fast, but Rosie is not one of them. So, not only are things whipping by on the highway in a way that's making Quag feel like he has to brace himself, but the whole car is trying to shake itself to pieces as they go. What happens if your car comes apart while screaming down a highway?

Not a good picture.

He asks her to slow down. She laughs like he is joking.

He's not joking.

"Mom," he says again. "Let's slow down a little, okay?" But she's batting his hand away and swerving around a van ahead. Past a pickup.

Once, when they first moved to Southton Falls, she had let him walk on the wooden railing of the pier that went out into the lake. She'd been in a spin; he'd been too little to know better, maybe. It had been fun. Her cheering him on from below. Him balancing, walking farther and farther out over the water, showing off.

It was only when he was almost all the way out to the tip that he had registered all the faces—his mom's face, excited, hands clasped above her head, but every other face below him, mouths open in terror. An old guy had reached up toward him, spoken to him gently. "Hey, little fella. Let me get you down from there, okay?" and for some reason (maybe all those faces?), Quag had leaned over and let himself drop into the old man's arms. He had felt the shake in those arms as the man lifted him down. "Where's your mama?" said the guy, who was suddenly holding on to Quag's arm too tight.

Even that young, Quag had known not to take him to his mom. He'd twisted out of the man's grip and run, dodging through all the legs on the pier until he got back to the park and reached the swing set. His mom had somehow found him there.

Quag has walked on the pier railing since. Usually late at night or just before a storm, when no one else was out there, and he could hear the halyards clanging against the masts of the sailboats moored off to the side. But he always hopped back onto the pier or turned around after the first two sections. Before some waitress watching from the restaurant next to the pier felt like she had to come out and yell at him to get-down-you-stupid-kid-are-you-trying-to-break-your-neck. Because Southton Falls pier is built on top of a bunch of riprap, and out near the tip, if you lean one way, you can just hop down onto the decking, but if you fall the other way, you'll fall at least twenty feet down onto sharp rocks.

They're stopped now. On the side of this road in this place where everything is flat. The road is flat. The sky is flat gray. The lines painted down the middle of the road lie flat. Like some construction guy walked along with limp, yellow rectangles hanging over his arm and slapped them down on the flat pavement all day long as he trudged west toward an end of the road that might not even exist. The only thing in the whole, stupid world that's 3D is Rosie, stopped on the side of the road. Blessedly, finally, still.

Quag lets out a shaky breath. Everything about him feels shaky right now. But there's his mom, big yellow purse still tucked under her arm, walking, quick and twitchy, across all four lanes of the highway and then off across the brown flat world to who knows where. Where is she going?

Quag jams his knuckles into the dashboard. He is so tired. So tired of this car. So tired of this trip to nowhere. So tired of following his mom. Feels like he's been following her his whole stinking life—down rickety stairs when they'd lost an apartment, through noisy restaurants, along school halls trying to get in front of her before she gets to the classroom and says something she shouldn't, into a car that's driving to the end of the world. So now, he's just supposed to follow her across the four lanes of this highway? Now, he's supposed to follow her across the brown grass? Follow her over the lip of the world?

Quag leans his head back against the seat and closes his eyes. He feels the air from a passing semi rock the car. What if he doesn't follow her? Another car zooms past, and he feels the question settle into his bones.

What if he doesn't follow her this time?

The heat outside the car is starting to seep in, even though they've only been stopped for a minute or something. He hauls his phone out of his pocket. Dead. Of course it's dead. Anyway, it's not like his mom would look at a text. Not like she'd explain where she's going. Explain that she'll be right back.

He chucks his cell phone into the cupholder near the gear shift and throws open the door of the car. The heat is immediate. So is the sound. Like a million bugs or something are making this blanket of sound. Like something out of an alien movie.

Another semi passes, and a hot wave of air hits him. He scoots across the first two lanes and down through the grass section in the middle, which is peppered with things left behind—a shredded tire, a red carton from a large fries, a hundred cigarette butts, beer cans, a lady's high-heeled shoe that looks like it used to be green satin but is now faded, half-buried in the dirt. Then he's waiting at the next bit of asphalt while a Jeep and a white pickup whiz by. He runs across the last two lanes of the highway. He can see his mom still marching resolutely along up in front of him.

How did they come to this?

Two weeks ago they'd been fine. Okay, his mom had lost her job at Bestin Plastics, and she thought Quag didn't know that. She told him they'd just changed her shift. Thought he didn't know that she cleaned the rooms at one of the dying hotels in one of the dying neighborhoods in Syracuse now. He knew. But they'd been okay.

And then they weren't. How can it be this easy to slide from okay to out of control? Nothing he has tried to get her to turn around, to get her to head back home, has worked. None of the things that usually work are working at all.

His mom is getting way out in front of him. He runs across the brown grass toward her, and now she's disappearing—yellow purse, quick walk—like somehow she's sinking into the ground, which can't be right. So this place must not be as flat as it seems from the road. All he can see now is her red hair and her shoulders marching themselves resolutely down and down until she's gone, leaving just the clamor of the bugs, and the getting-farther-away *whoosh* of cars going past, and the thud of his running feet.

And then he stops. Stops dead because he comes to a new world. A green world all laid out below him. A green world down in a wide ravine with a silver river curling through it. There are so, so many birds here. Wow. Birds swirl above the river, and wind whirls through tall green grass, stirring the blades so that they're now green, now silver, now green. And through this green world marches his mom.

The grass comes to Quagmire's shoulders down here, and birds fly up in bunches, like someone is throwing bird confetti in the air, as he walks through. The sky stretches over the grass like this is the whole world, like he could walk and walk, and he would swish through grass and birds forever maybe. He can see his mom ahead, still marching along in the middle of all this grass. He's not in a hurry to follow her.

Let her wait for him for a change.

If he stands still in this grass, it's quiet, just the wind whispering with the grass. And if he walks, it's noisy, all that bird confetti cussing him out as it flies and settles, flies and settles. So he stands still and feels the wind play with his hair like it's just another bit of grass, lifting it softly up, letting it fall, picking it up again, stirring it. If he stands here, maybe he will become grass. Maybe the birds will settle on him rather than around him. He'll feel the sun and the moon whirl above for days, for months, for years, until he can't remember anything but this—sun, wind, tiny bright-colored birds.

When he finally opens his eyes, he can't see his mom anywhere. Just this trail crushed through the tall grass where she walked. Where is she? How long has he been standing here? Why can't he see her? He should be able to see her.

He hurries down the path. The grass stands taller here. Surrounds him. Closes over his head. He jumps to see over it. To catch a glimpse of red hair.

Nothing.

"Mom?" he calls.

No answer.

He runs, his feet squelching into pockets of wetness under the grass. Around each turn, each twist of the path crushed in the grass, he expects to see the red hair bobbing along, the determined walk. But there's only the path. Empty.

"Mom?"

He crashes through, thrashing at the grass with his arms. The tall blades slice at him. She's nowhere.

And then he's falling. His face hits cold water. He spits and chokes and pushes himself up, gasping for air. "Mom!" he screams. He's knee-deep in a river, clear water running over gold sand scattered here and there with big chunks of broken concrete. "Mom!"

And there she is.

Fear crackles through him like ice is forming inside all his veins. Because there she is, a little upstream from him, stretched out between two jagged hunks of concrete like she would throw herself down on a bed after a long day, face up, her arms flung out to her sides. But this time she lies stretched out under the water. So still. Only her long red hair floating around her. The ice inside Quag freezes him where he stands, and he feels the roll of the earth around the sun creaking to a stop. The water slides by without making a sound. And Quag is so afraid.

Then his mom sits up and stretches her arms toward the sun and shakes her wet hair and laughs. She laughs. The ice that had frozen Quag melts in a rush, thawed by a ferocious anger. He lurches and stumbles toward her and drags her up out of the water until she stands, dripping, on her feet.

"What are you doing?" Quag screams at her. "What do you think you're doing?"

But she's still laughing. She grabs on to his arm like this is all a big joke, and she wants him to laugh with her. And the laughter tips him somehow. It's too much. The laughter makes him want to hurt her. None of this is funny.

"Are you crazy? You're crazy!" he yells at her.

He yanks his arm out of her grip and spins away from her. And as he does, she totters. She stumbles.

She falls.

SEVENTEEN

There is blood in the water—a thin snake of crimson threading out, winding around the concrete and into the river, where just a moment ago, his mom's hair had been floating. Quag drops to his knees next to her, reaching toward the gash on her head with one hand, trying to pull her up with the other. But she scuttles backward, and the fear in her eyes when she looks at him makes him raise both hands in the air to show her he means no harm. But somehow he knows—those eyes!—that no "I'm sorry, I didn't mean it" is going to fix this.

She has never looked at him like this before.

Her hand is going to her head, and when it comes away red, her look of disbelief is more painful to him than even her fear was. And then—and this only takes a second (how can it only take a second?)—she is a boiling whirlwind of fury. Words sluice out of her and wrap around Quag, hot and sharp and mean. She pushes herself up from the streambed, slapping away his offered hand, then jams her small fist into the middle of his chest to twist up a handful of his T-shirt and pull him toward the blistering heat of her words. Their edges feel like they leave welts on his face. These are her top-of-a-spin words. Things she would never say when she's okay. This is where she'll scream at him that he's ruined her life. This is where she'll tell him that he's always trying to keep her down. That he's making her life small. Small, small, small! He's trying to crush her!

When she pushes him away and, hand to head, stalks off through the path broken through the stems of grass, Quag knows not to follow her too close. He slumps there, eyes closed, and everything feels a little worse this time. Because this time he knows: He could have caught her if he'd wanted to. He'd let her fall.

Just this one time, he hadn't wanted to have to save her from herself. He'd been so angry with her. He'd let her fall.

Finally, he picks up her purse, gathering up receipts, Chap-Stick, and a purple pen that have fallen. He starts after her, trudging up through all that sea of grass. He's never let her get hurt before. Never. Not even in the middle of a full-rev spin, when he felt like his head would explode with her waves of endless talking, not when she blazed through the halls of a day churning up disaster. He'd had her back. Just like she'd had his—making under-her-breath comments about little dictators of tiny countries as they'd been ushered, for the third or fourth time that year, into Principal Deming's office. Saving him the leftover dough-nuts from meetings at her work and warming them up in the microwave after school for him, so when he walked in the door the glaze was soft and melty.

And now. The red trickling between her fingers . . . He'd done that. He'd let that happen.

The whole thing makes him feel sick.

He's climbing up out of the green now. The grass is shorter and deader, and he can hear the occasional car or semi whoosh by on the highway, even though he can't see the road yet. In one of the lulls, he hears a motor start, and he knows that motor. Rosie's motor, a little growlier than it should sound. The muffler's probably falling off again. He picks up his pace, because as mad as his mom is right now, if he makes her wait too long, everything will be worse.

Is she going to need stitches? Eric Yoon once ran into the crank on a volleyball post during gym, and he'd bled a lot too, and he'd needed stitches for the cut on his head. So if she needs stitches, don't they have to find a hospital? And then how are they gonna explain why she's soaking wet and has a cut on her head? You never know what will come out of her mouth when she's like this. He hears the motor rev as he climbs the slope of the ravine.

And as his head comes up over the lip, he sees the unbelievable sight of Rosie pulling away.

For three steps, five steps, eight steps, he runs, panic blooming through him. But it's too far. Something in him knows it's too far. The car is already a small blue blob wavering in the heat.

And then it's gone.

He stands in the grass, yellow bag hugged to his chest for a long time. He stands, waiting for a blue car to come back over the horizon. To come sliding to a stop, horn honking. Or to ease over to the side, tires crunching slowly over the gravel. He imagines it five different ways, willing the car to appear.

Nothing.

Nothing but an empty road and the hollow in his stomach that is more than hunger, more than fear. The hollow that means you're alone.

He'd thought he knew this feeling, had felt it before—in the hall at school, late at night when his mom was working graveyard. But he hadn't. Under that hollow, around it, his whole life there had been the *always* of his mom. Even when she'd gone missing those times, there was a rhythm to it. Somehow, he always knew she'd be back. There was some silver thread spun between them.

He knew. She'd spin down. She'd be back.

But this time?

This time, he doesn't know. He reaches down into that place where he's always known that she would come back, and he feels nothing. Just a hollow spot—dark, terrifying, wind blowing through it.

Quag waits for fifteen minutes, checking the time on the big pink plastic Minnie Mouse watch his mom keeps looped around her purse strap. She'll come back. Twenty minutes. She'll come back. Thirty. She has to get to the next exit and turn around. She'll come back. Forty minutes. Forty-two. Forty-seven.

She just drove off.

She fell. There was blood in the water.

She just drove off.

He let her fall.

She drove off.

What is he gonna do?

He backs off to a grassy hollow far enough from the highway that people will stop looking at him as they pass but he still has a view of the road. He lays out everything in the purse in a line. Like they're clues he can decode.

Some random letter. Useless. Her cell phone. Useless. Even if he gets somewhere where he could call her, now he can't call her. Big old wrench. Perfect. Look at all the things that need wrenching here in the middle of this grass that goes on as far as anyone can see. Couldn't be better. Wallet. Useless. Quag hid the cash and the debit card between the pages of the repair manual in the glove compartment. So that's turning out to have been a massively stupid idea.

He tries to call his own cell phone from hers, even though he knows his is dead in a cupholder in the car. Leaves a message she won't get. Leaves three texts she won't get. Call. Message. Text.

What is he gonna do?

She drove off.

This letter isn't even hers. It's for someone named Moira Mackleroy. His mom's name is Stefanie. Stefanie Tiarello. But it has the address of their apartment in Southton on it.

He slides his thumb under the flap, already unsealed. Pulls out some stiff, white paper. He sees the words Moira Stefanie Mackleroy. He sees the words "death of your father." He sees "will" and "bequest." There is a check for fifty-three dollars and nineteen cents inside the envelope.

Instructions. Addresses.

Moira Stefanie?

He can't understand any of this.

He reads the letter again.

A space is opening out in his brain. His mom is someone named Moira. She had a father. Fathers—hers, Quag's—are not something to discuss. She used to put her hands over her ears and walk out when Quag was little and wouldn't stop asking.

On the bottom of the letter there's a lime-green Post-it with handwriting on it. "Your brother is trying to reach you. Did not give him your information but promised to pass his number on to you in case you wanted to connect." A phone number.

Quag runs his finger over the number. A brother? So, Quag has an uncle?

A semi roars by on the highway.

Brother. Father. Moira.

There had been blood in the water. He pulled away; she fell.

She drove off.

What is he gonna do? What is he gonna do?

There had been so much blood in the water.

He punches the number from the Post-it into his mom's phone but doesn't press dial. The number comes up as "Jay." So has she already called him before this? Or just put him in her contacts?

Jay? His uncle?

What is he supposed to do? Text: "Hi. I'm your nephew. Also, small problem, I'm sitting in a ditch in the middle of nowhere?"

No.

No.

He turns the phone face down on the ground. Around him the grass starts to whisper. Leffft. Ffffffelll. Ssstefffanie. Leffft. Lossst.

His mom is not okay. She's alone. She's driving too fast.

He picks up the phone with shaking hands. Types "Jay" into her contacts. There's a number. There's an address in Nebraska.

Quag runs over his choices. He can't call anyone in Southton. All of those numbers are in his phone, not his head. And would he want to call Cassie about something like this? No. So then, call 911? Call this Jay person? Live on the side of the road for the rest of his life? He officially has zero good choices left.

He makes a decision. He presses dial.

EIGHTEEN

So this is turning out to be a crap Thursday, and the truck that pulls to the side of the highway over an hour later does not make Quag feel like it's going to get any better. It's old. Not cool old, like you sometimes see on summer nights in the parking lot of Clark's—old cars with big fenders and bright chrome that shine like someone has spent their whole life polishing those fenders every morning before breakfast and twice before they go to bed.

Nope. Just old. Like maybe a long time ago this pickup used to be pale blue but is now fading to white, except for the fender that has been Franken-trucked onto the right side and is the brown or orange or orange-brown of a shade from a long-ago decade.

The door on the far side of the cab opens. And all Quag sees are boots—first one, then another—descending onto the pavement on the other side of the truck. Cowboy boots. Like out of a movie. But with square toes. Buckles on the sides. Dusty and cracked, with the heels a little run-down.

The boots stop there on the other side of the truck, and, suddenly, those boots seem to Quag like something some random stalker who picks up kids off the sides of roads might wear. And

Quag is just today's victim. So maybe instead of standing here like an idiot, he should beat it back into the tall grass and try not to leave so much of a trail this time.

Because that's not like something out of a horror movie at all.

A text comes in a second after the boots come down: "That you in the red T-shirt?" Quag slides a fingertip over the thumbs-up, even though, technically, the fact that this is the long-lost (though apparently not rich) uncle does not erase the possibility that he's also a murderer, and is Quag really planning to get in that truck with him?

The man starts toward him. Uncle man is tall. Long, kind of gangly arms and legs and not much meat on the bones, except that when he walks out from behind the truck, Quag sees that this little paunch of a belly hangs over his belt buckle.

It's the belly that seems familiar to Quag. His mom has one of those, and then he wonders if all moms have one of those and that's not exactly enough of a family resemblance to bet your life on. But now the man is walking toward him, and there's something about the walk too, a kind of swing and shuffle to it, that seems familiar. And maybe if this guy's unruly hair was dyed red and there was more of it, it would look like his mom's kind of hair.

Or maybe he's making this all up.

And then, as if the guy knows what Quag is thinking, he stops and holds his hands up, the backs toward Quag. And there they are—the weird pinkie fingers bent at a ninety-degree angle, exactly like his mom's.

"Your mom got little fingers like this?" the man asks.

Quag nods.

"What's her favorite song?"

"'Chain of Fools.'"

"Still? I didn't even think that was a good choice when she was sixteen."

Quag's with him on that. Never got why anyone would like that song. But his mom does. Likes dancing around the kitchen singing the "ch-ch-chain" part.

"Well, you look like her. You've got her eyes." The man drops his hands to his sides and blows out a long breath. "She goes by Stefanie now, huh?" He looks around him at the highway and then Quag and kicks at a tuft of grass with his dusty boot. A sleek black car zooms past. The heat pours over them.

The man runs a big hand over his forehead. "She just left you here?" he asks. Like he's still trying to understand it all.

He is completely not buying Quag's story—that his mom was running late for a visit with a friend, so she dropped Quag off, asked him to call Jay and see if he could stay with him. That she'd pick him up from Jay's house in a couple of days.

Honestly, if uncle man had bought that, Quag would have no respect for him at all. It was the best Quag could do under the circumstances. The circumstances being that his own mom ditched him on the side of a road, that she is spinning hard. Not exactly the sort of thing you want to be discussing with someone you just met, even if he is some long-lost relative no one bothered to tell you about.

Quag shrugs and meets uncle man's eyes. When you bluff,

bluff big. "She was in a hurry. Told me to drop a pin, and you'd pick me up. I thought she'd already talked to you about it." Quag gestures to the grass around them. "Anyway, it's not like there's a ton of drop-off choices around here."

Uncle man gives him a brief, sharp look. Yeah, he is not buying any of this. But he doesn't say anything, just nods toward the truck.

It's a relief. Now Quag won't have to try to explain. To explain the fall, explain what came before the fall in some way that could help uncle man understand. Because even with all that explained, maybe it doesn't make sense to Quag either.

She just drove off.

They both start toward the pickup. Uncle man climbs in on the side nearest the highway, and Quag, still holding the yellow purse, opens the door on the side near the grass.

The truck's so old, it doesn't even have separate seats. Just this kind of bench thing done up in brown plaid and with a stripe of red duct tape running slantways across the seat back. In the middle of the seat is this sad-looking dog, all droopy ears and bags under his eyes. The dog raises his head, thumps his tail once on the seat like that's all he can manage, and then lowers his head back down onto his paws with a sigh. Quag scoots in beside him.

His uncle starts up the truck and flips on the AC, which Quag doesn't expect to do much, but it does. Sweet cold air washes across his bare arms as that big cowboy boot presses down on the gas pedal and the truck eases back onto the highway. The mile markers start spooling by again.

His uncle drums his long fingers on the top of the huge steering wheel. And then he just drives for a while. "Well," he finally says. "This is a hell of a thing, kid."

And Quag doesn't say anything, because that pretty much sums it up.

BIRDS: ENDURANCE

A common swift can stay in the air for ten months. Months. Scientists put trackers on them, and some of the birds didn't land once during all that time. They're fast enough to drink falling raindrops. They snatch insects out of the air. Somehow they sleep as they fly.

Ten months is a long time to stay up.

A really long time.

NINETEEN

They drive out of the tall grass and into the corn. So much corn, stretching out on either side of what is now a two-lane road. Uncle man doesn't say anything. What is he supposed to say? How's your day gone so far? Nice T-shirt? Where is your mom really?

And then Quag can ask, Been living in Nebraska long? What was your name again? Do you regularly pick up nephews you've never met from the side of the road, or is this a first for you too?

There's a lot of corn here. Just corn and this tunnel of a road running through it. The rumble of the engine thrums up through the soles of his feet and into his legs. He digs his fingertips into the rough fabric covering the truck's seat. This corn is messing with his head—rows and rows flicking past the window—*flick, flick, flick.*

What if he guessed wrong? *Flick, flick.* What if his mom isn't headed to Uncle Jay's house? *Flick, flick.* Sometimes when she spins, she'll take off to visit some random person—a friend she knew when she lived in Boston, someone she used to work for in Florida. It could have been Jay she was headed toward. *Flick, flick, flick.* Or not. *Flick, flick.* Such a long shot. What happens if she doesn't show up at uncle man's? *Flick, flick, flick, flick, flick, flick, flick.*

Quag closes his eyes against the corn.

When he opens them again, it's because there's the sound of wind pushing against the truck. They have come out of the corn into what feels like emptiness—the land stretching away and away and away in low hills covered by grass—grass that ripples like the water in the lake back home when the wind drives hard across it. And over all of this arches an endless sky of washed-out blue.

A train track runs alongside the road and twice, three times, a three-eyed monster of a train comes toward them on those tracks—always the two orange engines pulling brown cars, always the cars piled with coal, always the same pile, heaped in the same way in each car so that they remind Quag of a plastic train he used to have when he was little—a face painted on it and fake plastic coal piled in the back. He used to run his thumb back and forth over the bumpiness when he wanted to think about something.

Now they're passing through a handful of houses huddled along the tracks. Not arranged along real streets or anything. Like someone ran their car off the road at this point or that and plunked down a house. Small houses. Even the ones that are trying to have two stories can't quite commit to it. More like one story but with a gable or two cut through the roof. Like it might be dangerous to be too tall here.

Why are there no bushes around the houses? No yards really. Just dirt and houses and every house with some piece of rusty equipment out front, like it's some agreed-upon thing. *Nobody plant flowers. We're doing broken equipment, got it?*

No, wait. This house has headstones. Like you'd see in a yard around Halloween, except it's not Halloween, and these look like the real deal, not Styrofoam ones from Target. A faded plaque tacked to the side of the house spells out "Get your monuments here" in swirly letters, and some of these headstones have names already on them. Are they just waiting for some Cartwell or Johnson to kick off, so somebody will stop by for the stone on their way back from a grocery run?

Even the signs along the road are strange: "Charolais bulls, sale this Saturday." "Bison meat, quantity discounts." A blue-and-white sign with an arrow and an icon of a tree with a picnic table under it. Perfect. He's in a place where a tree is some kind of big attraction. He turns his head in the direction the arrow points. Can't see any tree.

How far would someone drive to see a tree?

There are birds even without the trees. Flocks of these intensely black birds with bright red patches on their wings flit up from the side of the road. A hawk sitting up on a fence post drops into the grass nearby, claws out. Something down there just bought the farm. Get your monuments here.

Everything leans toward brown. Brown dirt roads leading to brown houses. Brown mixed into the green of the endless grass stretching on either side of him. When Jay finally says, "Here we are," and they pull off the road and bump down a lane to a house that is legit two stories and painted white (even if the paint is chipped) and has a couple of scraggly bushes on either side of the door and an attempt at a square of lawn, Quag feels a strange wash of relief.

But only for a second.

There is no blue car in the driveway.

Of course there isn't.

TWENTY

Quag shuts the door of his bedroom-for-now. It's clearly used as kind of a storage room usually, since his uncle had to lift about fifteen boxes of old magazines with names like *Ag Quarterly* and *Husker Harvest* off the bed before they could get to it. The boxes are piled in the corner, and his uncle has gone back downstairs after awkwardly asking if he needs anything.

Yeah. Let me know if you see any missing moms.

Quag drops his mom's yellow purse next to the wall. Nothing to unpack. Pretty sure uncle man noticed that little detail. And the purse. Kind of tough to miss the purse. Doesn't exactly match up with his story.

He crosses to the window. This part of Nebraska is not flat. Hill after hill after hill piled against each other, like they're waves breaking on waves, and all of it covered by that weird grass— rippling, folding, twisting like it's alive. Alive in a way that you'd want to think twice about stepping out into it.

Well, he's not staying here in the land of freaky grass. Nope. He'll find his mom. Make sure they've got enough gas money to get back to Southton. Then he's out of here.

He needs a plan. He's good at plans. He's always been good at plans. But the part of his brain that can step back and make a plan is crashing around wildly inside his head. Where is she? Crash. Is she okay? Crash. She ditched him. Crash. She left. Crash. She left him on the side of some road.

He let her fall . . .

What had even happened down there by that river? That whole thing was so messed up.

A shuffling in the hall, and then a thump against the door. When Quag opens it a couple of inches, that sorry-looking dog from the truck is lying on the hall floor, right up against the door. The dog tilts his head to take Quag in.

This dog has the saddest eyes in the world. Legit. If they had a contest and brought in every single depressed animal on the planet, no one would even have to look twice before handing the blue ribbon to this dog. You could sell twelve-second sessions with this dog if you needed to bring people down from being too happy at their own weddings.

The dog gets to his feet. Does not improve his looks at all. Someone put the wrong size legs on this dog. Full-size dog, half-size legs, double-size paws. Like someone made a dog joke from what was left in the bottom of a scrap bin.

The dog stands in the hall like he's expecting something to happen.

What does he want?

Quag opens the door wider. The dog clicks past him, into the room, and over to the bed, where he stops and waits.

No way.

The bed is Quag's.

Quag closes the door and crosses the room. "Not happening, buddy," he says. The springs creak as he sits. He lays down and stares at the ceiling. Tries to slow his brain down. He needs a plan.

For just a second, in that truck driving through the middle of nowhere, Quag had thought about telling his uncle the truth. *So, about your sister. She is not visiting a friend. She's spinning hard, and she just drove off, and I have no clue where she is or where she's going.*

But he couldn't. Like when he opened his mouth to say it, he just couldn't. He never talks to anyone about his mom. Telling will make things worse.

When she comes down a little, she'll be back to get him. She always comes back.

But now his stupid brain is revving up and hitting all the walls again. Will she think to look for him here? Will she go back to where she left him? Back to New York? Will she even remember where she left him? Is she going to be okay? She's worse this time. It doesn't go like this usually. What if she doesn't come back? Crash, crash, crash.

Come on, come on. This should be simple. Make a plan. Mom, money, gone.

There's a low huff from the side of the bed, and the dog, with a laborious heave, lifts his two front paws onto the quilt near Quag's shoulder. He stands there, back feet still on the floor, front feet on the mattress, and huffs again. Then he lays his muzzle between his paws and nudges at Quag's arm.

Quag had thought that when people drew cartoons of these kinds of dogs, they'd been exaggerating. If anything, they hadn't gone far enough. The eyes are deep wells of sorrow—like somehow every sad thing that's ever happened in the world has been seen by this dog, and now he has to carry all that around all day, and nothing can ever make him happy again.

Quag scrambles up and heaves the sorry dog onto the bed and lies back down next to him. Sad Dog sighs and stretches and settles into the quilt. And when he plops his ridiculously heavy head onto Quag's chest, Quag doesn't push him off.

When Quag comes down from the bedroom a while later, an old laptop is sitting on the kitchen table. Quag listens for the sounds of someone else being in the house. Nothing.

He opens the computer. Gets in easy. Doesn't even have a password.

Who doesn't have a password on their computer?

Quag checks his mom's social media accounts. Nothing. Checks her bank account. Nothing. Then he googles whether he can track the position of his cell phone if the cell phone is dead. That looks like a no. You can only track where it had been when it went dead, and he already knows where that was because he had been there.

How is he going to find his mom? His phone (dead) is with his mom. His mom's phone died somewhere between the middle of nowhere side of the road and the middle of nowhere ranch. How's he supposed to do anything without a phone?

He needs a charger. He logs into his mom's Amazon account and puts one in the cart. She has her card saved to the account, so there's at least that. But where is he? He pulls an envelope from a stack of bills on the counter and types in the address. Same day delivery is not a thing here. It's going to take three days.

Great.

He should get into Jay's email. See if his mom ever emailed Jay or not. If she did, then maybe she really is coming here. But as he opens the email, he hears the screen door creak. He stands up from the table so fast he knocks over the chair with a bang. He hears the door clatter shut. Footsteps in the hall.

Log out of email, log out of browser, get chair back on its feet. He's standing at the cupboard, taking down a glass when Jay walks into the room.

But he didn't have time to clear the history. And after he drinks his glass of water and turns back around, the laptop has disappeared from the room. Not good. That chair going over was sloppy. The envelope still sitting on the table was sloppy. Not clearing the history was sloppy.

He wishes he'd had time to clear the history.

TWENTY-ONE

This is what happens the morning after you end up in the middle of nowhere with an uncle you didn't know you had. You learn to feed calves. Because your uncle says you both need something to keep your minds busy.

And this is the thing he picks?

Don't even ask. It does keep your body busy, trying to make sure this big, heavy, white plastic bottle doesn't end up in the straw on the barn floor, and that you don't end up squashed against the fence, and your sneaker doesn't end up in a pile of poop, and your shirt doesn't end up covered in calf snot. But your mind will not be too much needed.

It's free to wander. Or to run around the rutted track of where is she, where is she, where is she, where is she? Quag works hard to keep it from jumping that track, because he can feel the shape of the next question that his mind wants to scramble toward, and he won't think that, he can't think that, he won't.

So, feed the calves, morning and evening, go to sleep on the creaky bed in the upstairs room, get up, work hard to keep your mind on nothing while you put on the new clothes your uncle picked up from Walmart, eat, feed the calves, shower, don't think, don't think, don't think.

And while you're busy not thinking, you will be accidentally interrupting conversations your uncle is having on his phone. Because he's clearly drawn some conclusions, even though Quag hasn't told him a thing, and in the past two days, Jay has spent hours on the phone, a lot of them with a buddy of his who's a retired cop. Quag had come into the kitchen this morning, and his uncle was standing, his forehead against a cabinet, listening to whoever was on the other side of his phone and saying, "I know, I know. But if I call her in . . . I just don't want her to lose her kid." And then seeing Quag in the doorway, he'd said, "Gotta go."

He'd tucked the phone, with its cracked screen and battered black case, into the pocket of his plaid shirt. "Hungry?" he'd asked Quag. And although Quag was hungry, ravenously hungry for some reason, Quag said, "Nope," and left.

He wanders down behind the barn and takes off into the grass. He's starting to hate the grass around here. With all its *whisper, whisper, whisper.* Like it thinks it knows all your secrets. But there aren't a lot of choices. Grass, barn, house, or road to nowhere. He wades through the stupid, whispering grass until he comes to a little stream, cutting bright through the field.

Beside that stream stands a bird.

Not a bird like a back-home bird. Not a little gray-brown thing that pecks at pieces of leftover pizza crust, or a sketchy-looking duck that swims laps in a fountain, or even a directionally challenged sea gull.

This bird is big, almost as tall as Quag, long-legged and long-necked and covered with long gray feathers, ruffling in the wind. A beak like a murder weapon outlined against the sun. The bird stands looking out over the stream, and as it swivels its head toward Quag, something in Quag's belly goes weak—the front of the bird's head is red with blood. No, his stomach is getting itself back together, because it isn't blood at all, just a brilliant patch of red feathers splashed across the front of the gray face. And the eyes—round, gold, giving no quarter.

The way that bird looks at him reminds him of the way Cassie looks at him sometimes. Like she is expecting something from him, who knows what, like she's annoyed with him for taking so long to get to it. The bird stares at him like that.

This bird probably used to be a dinosaur way back. It has black, scaly feet fitted out with claws that would look just right in a dinosaur movie, and maybe you want to stay away from those feet and from that dinosaur beak, which probably doesn't still have teeth in it, but you'd hate to be wrong about that up close like this. So close that Quag can see the slash of a big hole for breathing in that polished spear of a beak, can see the velvet of the scarlet feathers, and the deep black pupil of a golden eye.

What does the bird see through those eyes?

The bird looks at him. Quag doesn't move. You don't move while the universe is deciding about you.

And then the bird turns back toward the stream and stalks the three steps down to the bank. The bird walks like a king, like it doesn't care one way or the other whether Quag is there. Like

Quag is too inconsequential a thing to even acknowledge.

Quag feels an empty spot open up inside his chest, and he turns and heads back out of the grass toward the house. Not because he cares what some stupid bird thinks. Not because he wants to be in the house with this Uncle Jay person he didn't even know about until two days ago. Not because there will be any comfort there. Just because the world seems so lonely that he can't stand it.

TWENTY-TWO

Here are some bad surprises about country living. First, people get up earlier than any people should ever get up for anything. Second, milk. Quag's not a fool. He knew it came out of a cow. But he hadn't thought much about it. Now that he's a little more acquainted with the process, he may be off milk for the foreseeable future. This morning he poured Dr Pepper on his cereal, which was not great but also had not come out of a cow.

Another bad surprise is that everything you get up at o'dark thirty in the morning to do, you'll have to do all over again later in the day. Every single day. And if you have even an inch of sock showing above your sneakers, after you walk through the grass, that inch will be full of these sticker things that will take you forever to pick out.

The sunsets are okay though. If you like that kind of stuff.

There is a sandhill crane with dinosaur feet stalking around down by the creek. Not sure if that's a good thing or a bad thing, but it definitely gets your attention.

And Jay has a horse here. Which, okay, horses are way big in person. Like, so big that if this horse (her name is Claire) decided to, she could take a chunk out of the top of your head with her big horsey teeth, or clobber you into confetti with her big horsey feet, or mash you into a little smear of jelly against the side of her stall, because she weighs like a hundred times more than you do. Don't even kid yourself that the tiny rope that Jay leads her out of the stall with would do anything if she didn't want it to.

The weird thing is, she doesn't do any of those things. She's just kind of chill about being bigger and stronger than anybody else in the barn. The first time Quag stopped to look at her in her stall, she wandered over and pushed her huge nose gently against the front of his shirt. Just checking him out. And then she tipped her head a little and looked at him out her deep brown eyes like she was saying, "So. Tell me about your day." And he didn't, because Jay was just down the way. But he could have. He somehow felt like she would have gotten it.

"I see you're on Claire's approved list," said his uncle, walking past. And Quag had no idea what being on that particular list meant, but it felt okay. Maybe more than okay.

It's so quiet here. No cars going past his bedroom window at night. No one yelling. Nothing but the wind outside doing its *whisper, whisper* till it starts to seem like if you stand and listen real careful for just a few minutes more, maybe you'll finally understand what it's saying.

But the quiet *inside* the house is stressing Quag out. The words-per-hour count in this house is about 2.5. "Hungry?" "Bologna, okay?" "Let's head out." This is about a thousand words per hour less than Quag's mom operates at, and, okay, his mom can get to be a bit much, but Jay's version is worse. Every hour Quag's in the house, the silence seems to swell and press itself further into the corners of every room, seems to crush up against Quag's throat. It feels impossible to say, "So about my mom . . ." It's starting to feel impossible to say anything at all.

So, today, when Jay says, "Heading into town on an errand. Want to come, or would you rather stay here?" not only blowing his words-per-hour stats completely out of the water for the day, but stringing two whole sentences together, Quag is so surprised that he opts in. Not that he's looking forward to spending more silent time with uncle man in that fab truck of his, but because if you're planning on getting out of a place, you need to understand your nearest escape routes.

There is one road. One road leading into town. The same road leading out. And "town" seems to be a word that's more wishful than descriptive. Quag swivels around looking for a bus or an Amtrak station, and it doesn't take him more than twelve seconds to be pretty sure he's not going to find either here.

There is a church. And that seems to be where Jay is heading. The wild thought that maybe they have orphanages attached to churches here like they sometimes do in old books flashes through Quag's brain. Because if his mom was supposed to be back from "visiting her friend" in a "couple days," that would have been yesterday.

Wow.

Get a grip, Tiarello. It's Sunday. Some people go to church on Sunday.

But he is surprised. Jay hadn't struck him as a church kind of guy. And church isn't exactly a Tiarello family specialty, but aren't you supposed to dress up? Because neither of them are anything remotely like dressed up.

This church looks serious. All brick and stone. Big steps up to quadruple doors. A huge arched window. Five-story tower with this fancy stone bit on top with arches and spire things and maybe a bell in there and the whole bit. None of this low-to-the ground stuff for this church, though the houses clustered around it are not so brave.

But they're not stopping at the church itself. They're pulling around on a sandy lane that curves behind the church, parking in front of a rectangular white building with a metal roof, and Quag's following Jay into a little door in the side of the building. They enter the sound of a room full of people talking.

Quag is used to people taking notice when he walks into a room. He walks into a classroom at school, the teacher is immediately aware and watching. The other kids sit up, waiting to see what will happen. When he walks into Snarkey's, the guy who runs the cash register is tracking him as soon as he comes through the door. Quagmire Tiarello is here. Pay attention.

Something like that happens when they walk into this room full of people sitting around on folding chairs at rectangular tables, eating. But it's not Quag they're noticing. It's Jay. And what happens in the room is not a wariness, not a waiting to see. It's more like a smile sweeping across the room. Nods and waves. A woman motions Jay over to a table full of food and starts talking trash to him about people who time their arrival to miss the preaching but not the food, but she's also grinning so big, the smile lines around her eyes make deep crinkles, and she's filling up two thick paper plates as she jaws at him.

How is some guy who never talks friends with all these people?

The food lady smiles at Quag as she puts the heavy plate into his hands, like, whoever he is, she's happy to see him too. Quag's glad of the plate with its big bun filled with meat and barbeque sauce, with its potato salad, with its baby carrots with a blob of ranch dressing, with the little bag of sour-cream-and-onion chips balanced on top. Uncle Jay is a chili-out-of-a-can guy. Even three days of can chili is a lot.

And Quag is glad of the smile. It somehow loosens something inside his chest. But it feels weird to not have people notice that he walked in.

To know nothing about him.

It's been a long time since that happened.

He wonders what it feels like to be Jay. To have everyone notice you, but in a way that doesn't expect you to do anything. Isn't looking to you to make class less boring on a slow Wednesday. Isn't hoping you'll get in someone's face, so people will have something to talk about in the hall.

Jay winds his way through the tables, nodding as people call out his name, but he's clearly headed someplace. That place is the back corner of the room, where a tall girl in a dark blue jacket, with a bunch of patches on one side and some big gold seal kind of thing sewn on the other, sits with her boots propped up on the folding chair beside her and her hands behind her head. She has her hair looped into a loose ponytail, and her face is speckled with a bunch of splotchy freckles. She's older than Quag—high school, for sure—and she watches both of them as they come toward her, her eyes traveling back and forth between them, so that by the time they get to her table, Quag feels like she has all the information visually available about both of them and has made some decisions.

Quag doesn't like it.

"Hey," says Jay, settling down across from her. "Your mom told me I'd find you here."

"Gran wanted to come, but she refuses to drive anymore," says the girl. She's still watching Quag, and he sees her note the empty chair he leaves between him and Jay as he sits down.

None of her business where he sits.

"Right," says Jay, and takes a bite of his sandwich and sits quiet until he's done chewing. "This is my nephew, Quagmire Tiarello," he says.

The girl turns her eyes back toward Quag and raises an eyebrow. "Quagmire?" she asks. "That the name your mama gave you, or that some sort of nickname?"

Stupid question. Why would your own mom name you Quagmire?

In fifth grade, when he was still named Quentin, this jerk substitute named Mr. Barry had called him a "quagmire of ignorance," and written the definition of *quagmire* on the board, and made this whole big deal of it. So Quag had just signed his name as Quagmire Tiarello to every worksheet the sub handed out that week and turned it in blank. He'd worn the name like a dare, just to see the flush of anger every time the sub saw it. The other kids thought it was funny, and Quag got the kids in his class, and then everyone else, to call him Quagmire.

His mom had nothing to do with that name. This girl is stupid to even think it.

Jay clears his throat. "Quagmire's staying with me for a while," he says. "I'd like you to train him to help you in the barn."

Is anyone going to ask Quag what he thinks about this plan?

There's a pause while everyone does some more chewing. Apparently not. And usually Quag would make a big deal about it, or at least refuse to show up, but he's kind of in a touchy spot—a missing mom who was supposed to be here yesterday and all.

"Nice," says the tall girl, finishing off one of the little bags of chips. "I can always use another hand in the barn." And then she and Jay are talking about FFA (whatever that is) and some trip to Grand Island (wherever that is) that she just got back from.

Quag watches as people wander by to say hi to Jay, who turns out to be a decently chatty guy when he's not at home. (So he only doesn't talk to Quag?) People stop to ask him random questions about cows that are having issues, to see what he thinks about a town council thing that will be going to a vote next week, or just to shoot the breeze. They all give the tall girl a nod and a greeting too. They ask how she and her horse did at some competition last week. No one seems surprised that she won in two events and got second in another. So in her case, the goodwill isn't just spillover from Jay. Whoever she is, she commands her own brand of respect.

TWENTY-THREE

On Monday, uncle man leaves Quag in the barn with the older girl from church and heads out. To check on some fences, he says. Like a fence is going to go somewhere.

"Hey," says the girl. She reminds Quag of Rhia, in a way. Not that they look alike, other than the fact that they're both taller than him and built solid, but just in the way they both seem so comfortable doing whatever they're doing. In this case, shoveling a bunch of horse poop into a wheelbarrow, but whatever. It's like they've staked out their place in the world and expect the whole world to just fold itself around them.

"You got boots?" asks the girl. Quag doesn't answer, because it's kind of obvious that he doesn't, and he thinks she can pretty much see that.

"Tell Jay you need boots," says the girl. "Or you're going to have all kinds of crap stuck in the laces of those tennis shoes. Besides, Helga"—she gestures toward a spotted cow licking up some hay with a pink tongue—"likes to step on people and break their feet."

Perfect.

"Also, sorry for what I said about your name yesterday. That was out of line. Your name's your name." She leans on the pitchfork she's been using and looks him over. "My name's Maggie. Maggie Loomis."

Like Quag cares.

"So we're planning on working in companionable silence, I see," she says. "Your call. I apologized. Do with it what you will."

She hands him the pitchfork and walks over to a bunch of tools hanging from hooks on the wall and gets down another. Picks up a pair of gloves from a bin on her way back and holds them out to Quag.

He shakes his head.

"Oh, a tough guy," says Maggie. "Great. Love the tough guys." She shies the gloves back toward the bin, and they land squarely inside. "Get shoveling, tough guy."

Quag thinks about not shoveling. This isn't his stupid farm. But somehow, she's giving the impression that she couldn't care less whether he does or he doesn't, and that makes it feel like not shoveling would come off as weak. Pretty sure he can shovel as much horse crap as this Maggie Loomis can.

He starts out matching her rhythm—scoop, toss, scoop, toss. It's not like this is super complicated. Not like this is something he needs some high school chick to train him how to do. He scoops a little faster. Maggie smoothly matches his speed. Quag speeds it up again. Maggie glances at him and matches. And then after a minute of them shoveling together, she looks over at him, one eyebrow raised and a crooked grin on her face, and speeds it up again.

Quag does not appreciate the grin. He speeds up to match.

It only takes him about ten minutes to wish he'd taken the gloves.

It is impossible to get out of here.

The Amazon box with the charger was on the kitchen table when Quag got in from the barn, and Jay gave him a look but didn't say anything. Now, phone still plugged into the wall, Quag's scrolling through the options on a website that shows all the ways you can get from one place to another. It takes five separate Greyhound buses to get from here to home. Or one bus and then two trains. And even then, it's an hour and a half to the nearest bus station, so that's going to take a car. Or twenty-six hours and seven minutes of walking, as the site helpfully points out. In case you're wondering.

Uber doesn't work here. Even if he had money for that. Like it just doesn't exist. No taxis. Couldn't be better.

Anyway, he's got to find his mom first. And that's a way bigger problem. There is no site for conveniently locating missing moms.

BIRDS: CHICKENS

Chickens are straight-up weird. At first, you think they're not that smart. Because they seem like they're just wandering aimlessly around talking to each other all the time. All the time—like they are the chatty drama kids of birds with the constant cluck, cluck, clucking. They get overexcited about stuff like the drama kids do too. Bring out some cracked corn and see how that goes. Full-out chicken frenzy.

There's even this way-out-there chicken that's like a Mikey chicken—weird is its brand—blue feet and this wild feather pom thing on its head that's so big, you wonder how it can see. Maybe that's why all the other chickens are talking all the time: "Hey, Mikey, don't walk into the wall. Food's over here, Mikey. Nope, nope, a little to your left."

But then today, some mouse or something went running across the floor in front of the chickens, and they instantly went all mighty hunter in a way that was legit scary. It was like one second, they were these sleepy, goofy birds only interested in scratching up a dust-covered snack, and then the next second, there was this little pack of feathered velociraptors thundering down the barn aisle chasing down a mammal in their territory and doing some bloodlust thing.

Made you glad you are substantially bigger than the chickens.

TWENTY-FOUR

Quag wakes up in a rush. It's light already. He's going to be late for ArtCamp. A gentle wheeze next to him. There's a dog on his bed. There's a quilt that looks like it was covered with roses three hundred washes ago.

The mild panic of "late" ramps up into something serious within seconds. He feels like someone is standing on his chest. His lungs aren't working. He can't get enough air into them.

No ArtCamp.

No Foley box.

No Cassie.

No Mom.

He can't breathe right.

His whole body hurts. From the pitchforking yesterday. So stupid. Rolling over hurts. Staying still hurts. His hands hurt.

He's aware that he should be happy that no one woke him up and dragged him out to the barn this morning. But waking up not knowing where he is, everything in his life missing, is worse. So much worse. He doesn't want to be in this room. He doesn't want to be on this farm. He needs to go home.

In the kitchen, Jay's wallet and keys aren't on top of the refrigerator where he leaves them when he's in the house. Quag fills up the bowl from the container of dog food stored in a garbage can on the porch for Sad Dog, who is actually named Ollie apparently, and heads out to the barn. Because he can't stand being in the house.

Jay's not in the barn either. But Maggie is.

"You okay?" says Maggie when he comes in.

He's not okay. That not-being-able-to-breathe-right thing this morning is freaking him out. That's never happened before. What was that?

"I'm fine," he says.

"That the answer you would give a friend?" asks Maggie.

Why is this any of her business?

"No," says Quag.

"Okay," says Maggie. "Good to know where I stand." She leans back and looks him over. When her eyes drop to his hands, Quag makes fists, even though that hurts a lot. "Come here," she says, propping her pitchfork against the wall and heading down the barn walkway. "Come here, come here, come here."

And Quag follows her. Probably because he's too tired to make coherent decisions. She ends up in a little room that has two saddles on sawhorses and a whole crap ton of other horsey, leathery stuff hanging from the walls.

"Lemme see," she says, nodding toward Quag's hands. When he doesn't respond, she raises an eyebrow. "Seriously, kid. Show me the hands."

He turns his hands palms upward, and she lets out a low whistle.

"Impressive," she says, and she's already on the move, hauling a bin down from a shelf. "Wash," she says, nodding toward the grubby sink attached to the wall. "Wash gently. With this." She holds out a bottle from the bin.

Quag doesn't take it.

Maggie sets the bottle down on the sink with a thump. "Kid, is it your personal policy in life to make every little thing harder for yourself? See that blister down by your thumb that's popped and that's hurting like all get-out?" Quag is aware of this blister. And it is hurting like all get-out, if hurting like all get-out means hurting a lot. "Every single other blister that you've managed to raise on both of your hands, which looks to me like somewhere between five and seven more, is going to pop during the next hour if we don't do something about this. So love me or hate me, but you don't need that. And I don't need barn help that can't help. Wash."

Quag washes. Gently, as instructed.

When he finishes, he turns to find Maggie cutting what looks like a bunch of little doughnut shapes out of some pinkish, spongy-looking stuff. "Hand," she demands. He holds out his hand.

So what's up with that? Now he's just going to do anything Maggie says to do?

But her touch, as she starts to peel the backs off the little dough-nut shapes she's cut out and position them around each of the blisters, is gentle. It makes him feel weird to have her touching his hand. Not like he feels when Cassie bumps her shoulder against his or sits next to him, not like something in him is floating. It's nothing like that at all. It's just . . . well, he just met her. And he didn't like her. Might have hated her. Because of that whole business about his name. And she gets that—he's made it pretty clear—but she's just matter-of-factly fixing up his hand anyway.

"Other hand." He holds out his other hand, and Maggie finishes and then brushes the little paper backing pieces into an empty calf feed canister that she's apparently decided is now a garbage can. "Okay. So that should keep the pressure off the blisters and keep them from rubbing. But I think you should feed those two calves instead of mucking out. If you brace the bottles against your belly and just keep them where they need to be using your fingertips, you shouldn't rub against the blisters too much. I'll put the bottles together, and then you can take over. That work?"

And something about her straightforward way of asking makes Quag say, "Yeah, that works." When she walks by as he's starting over toward the calf pens and, without a word, in that same matter-of-fact way, hands him a pair of gloves, Quag carefully puts them on.

Ollie is sitting in the barn aisle looking up at a plastic Rubbermaid cabinet screwed to the wall again. He's done this every day Quag's been here. It's empty except for a rope and a couple of horse brushes. Quag checked. So what's up with the dog?

"Move it, Ollie," says Maggie, trying to scoot around him while carrying a bale of hay. Ollie does not move it. Maggie drops the bale next to Quag with a thump. "Jay used to keep the dog treats there," she says. "But the mice got into the box. Ollie can't quite get over hoping. Look, Olls. Empty." She opens the cabinet to show him. Ollie is undeterred. He wags his tail, hopeful. Maggie shrugs. "They're in the house now. We'll get him one once we're done."

And they do. But something about Ollie sitting there every day, waiting for something that isn't ever going to happen, bothers Quag. He wanders back to the barn and pulls an empty plastic feed supplement jar with a twist-top lid out of the trash. He washes it in the kitchen sink, grabs a Sharpie from the junk drawer next to the refrigerator, writes *Good Dog* across the front, and fills it with dog treats.

That afternoon, when Ollie stations himself below the cupboard, Quag reaches in, unscrews the lid, and tosses Ollie a couple of treats. Ollie follows him around the barn, from chore to chore, after that. When his uncle brings home a bag of freeze-dried mealworms (apparently those are a thing), Quag adds a *Good Chickens* canister to the cupboard. Which means that by the end of the next day not only Ollie but the chickens (Mikey chicken's head pom bouncing along as it runs) have developed a little fixation with the cabinet.

"What have you done?" Maggie says as Quag tries to come past the cabinet with the wheelbarrow, stirring up a noisy tide of chickens. But Quag had seen her grin at the *Good Chickens* label earlier when she opened the cupboard to get down Claire's lead rope, and she's smiling now too.

When Quag opens the cabinet the next morning, there is a clear plastic deli container with *Good Quag* scrawled across the front in blue marker and three chocolate chip cookies inside. "Ha, ha," says Quag to Maggie, who is in Claire's stall with Jay while they do something that involves Claire's hooves and a wicked-looking hook thing. Claire stands there chewing like absolutely nothing is going on. But Quag is not about to pass up three chocolate chip cookies when breakfast was some kind of cereal that looked and tasted like he was eating miniature hay bales.

Quag gets into the house before Jay that night. Which is good, because Quag is so not having chili again. He uses up three-quarters of a loaf of bread making a whole stack of grilled cheese sandwiches and is sitting at the table eating his way through them when Jay comes in, fills up a mug with water from the sink, and sits down. "How are those blisters coming along?" Jay asks. He nods at the pink bandages on Quag's hands.

"Better," says Quag.

"Good. That's good," says Jay.

Jay takes a sip of his water and then rubs his knuckles back and forth against his forehead. It's a familiar movement. Quag's mom does that sometimes. When she's worried.

Silence except for the sound of Quag chewing.

"Hey, Quag?" Jay is running his finger around and around the edge of his cup now and not making eye contact.

Jay's going to ask about his mom. Quag knows it. "Want a sandwich?" asks Quag. He hops up, crosses to the stovetop, and starts putting together another grilled cheese without waiting for Jay to answer.

"Sure. Grilled cheese is always nice," says Jay, looking at him a little longer than is completely necessary, like he's trying to figure something out. "Why don't you let me take care of the dishes tonight, since you cooked" is what he finally says when Quag flips a couple of sandwiches onto a plate and hands it to him.

It's hard to get to sleep that night. It's Thursday. No wonder Jay wants to know what's going on. It's been seven days since that disaster by the side of the highway.

Where is his mom?

BIRDS: NEST

It's kind of wild that a bird that doesn't even have opposable thumbs can build a nest. Quag found this empty nest in a scraggly bush down by the creek, and it was beautiful. Perfect. You could hardly believe anything could make something that perfect. Quag thought about bringing the whole thing back to the house, maybe keeping it in one of the drawers of the old dresser so he could look at it some more. But maybe the birds come back and use it again. Who knows?

He found some pieces of shell in the grass too, shining blue through the brown and green, like a piece of the sky had fallen. But the thing is, you can't know what that means. Did the babies hatch and grow up in that perfect nest and then fly off, and now they're out there swooping around, having a good time? Or did a cat get them before they even had a chance?

You can't know.

TWENTY-FIVE

"You don't know how to drive a truck?" Maggie is looking at Quag like he just admitted that he doesn't know how to put on his own shorts.

Why would he know how to drive a truck?

Maggie continues like he said it out loud. "Everyone knows how to drive a truck, Quag. Everyone's been driving field roads since they could see over the dashboard. Kids your age will be driving themselves to school this year."

"I'm fourteen."

"Yeah!" says Maggie. "You can get a school permit when you're fourteen and two months." She digs her keys with their grubby yellow lanyard out of her pocket. "Come on," she says.

She thumps on the open door of the tiny messy room in the barn that serves as a kind of office for his uncle. "I'm going to teach Quag to drive the truck," she says as they go past.

You can drive when you're fourteen here?

"Stay on the field roads," yells Jay after them.

"Yeah, yeah," says Maggie.

How can you drive when you're fourteen here?

Maybe he doesn't need Uber to get to the bus station.

So. Turns out you don't have to crank the wheel as much as you do in video games. Like at all. The swerves strike Maggie as the funniest thing that has happened all day. And all Quag has to say about that is that since they've been mucking out stalls, funniest thing that's happened today is a pretty low bar. The laughing from the other side of the truck seems excessive, thank you.

Then, once he figures out the swerving, he goes too slow. So slow that it's like a tectonic plate instead of an engine is pushing the truck forward. When he tries to speed up, he snaps them both back against the seat and then flings them forward, trying to slow down. Maggie's huge grin is way irritating. "Make up your mind, kid," she says. "Don't just stomp on every pedal on the floor." But after that, with Maggie giving instructions (still laughing though), he does better—slow, but not embarrassingly slow, down the lane.

And then a little faster.

Faster. And straight.

He's doing good.

And then Quag sees it. A flash of blue. A flash of blue in the distance, coming along the road out at the end of the lane. Blue, the color of his mom's car, Rosie. He pushes the gas down and down. The tires slip then catch as the truck picks up speed along the lane.

"Too fast," says Maggie. "Slow it down."

But he can't.

He has to get out to the road before the car gets there. Has to let his mom know he's here. At Jay's. Has to make sure she sees him.

Maggie is yelling, her hand on his arm. He shakes her off.

He can get there.

He can get there before the blue car.

He's almost there.

And then Maggie has one hand on the steering wheel, and she's hauling up on some kind of lever thing in between the seats. The steering wheel shudders under his hands, and the truck skids and throws up a cloud of dust so big that it billows around them as they slide to a stop. But Quag is out of the truck, running through the dust, trying to see that blue through the dust, trying to get to that blue on the road before it's . . .

Too late.

The blue whips past. And as it goes by, he sees that it isn't Rosie at all. Just one of those mini-pickups. The same blue Rosie would have been if it had been Rosie. But it wasn't.

Quag hears tires crunch behind him.

"Get in," says Maggie, through the open window. Her splotchy freckles stand out starker than usual against her skin. She jerks her thumb toward the passenger side. "Get in."

Quag climbs in and slams the door. He stares out the window, watching the blue truck that isn't Rosie pick up speed along the long road leading away from the ranch.

"Want to explain what that was about?" says Maggie.

No. Quag does not want to explain what that was about.

Maggie does a quick turn in the road and heads back up the

lane, steering smoothly to miss ruts and hollows. When they pull up near the house, she puts the truck in park and flips the locks. "Want to explain what that was about?" she asks again.

Quag tries his door. He can feel Maggie looking at him. He stares out the window. Open the door, Maggie Loomis. No one wants to talk to you about this.

"Quag, if you're in some kind of trouble, Jay is pretty trusty," she says quietly.

"What would you know about it?" In the side mirror, Quag can still see the dust floating in the air back where Maggie wrestled the truck to a stop.

"I'm seventeen," she says. "Old enough to have been in some kind of trouble before."

What's that supposed to mean?

Doesn't matter. Quag doesn't want to talk to Maggie about this. His mom left him by the side of a road—maybe on purpose, maybe for no reason at all. He thought he just saw her. He didn't. Happy?

When Maggie finally unlocks the door, he's out of the truck, across the porch, and into the house. He almost crashes into Jay as he comes around the corner into the hall.

"Whoa," says Jay, flattening himself against the wall as Quag storms past. "You okay, kid?" Quag doesn't want to talk to Jay about this either. Maggie will tell him about it anyway. Quag doesn't want to talk to anyone at all. He bounds up the stairs to his room. Doesn't even let Ollie in that night.

TWENTY-SIX

A few hours later, the lightbulb above Quag's bed flares on. "Get up," says his uncle. "I need your help." It is deeply night outside the window, and all Quag can think of is that they must have found his mom, so he is throwing jeans on over his boxers and fighting his way into a shirt. He follows his uncle down the stairs in the dark.

The screen door clatters shut behind them, but instead of heading to the pickup, his uncle turns toward the barn, jog trotting, boots scuffing through the dust. So maybe it isn't his mom at all. "I need your help," Jay says again, and then he says something that Quag, still rattled from waking up in 1.76 seconds with a light blazing in his face, hears as "Claire's Foley," which makes no sense at all. Quag's brain is trying to puzzle it out as they come into the barn, where the lights are already on.

And there is Claire, standing in the big stall, sweat darkening her red coat until her sides are almost black. His uncle moves over to lay his hand along her neck. "Get the Foley box," he says to Quag. "It's in the feed room. Blue box on the shelf behind the door." And when Quag stands there, because probably this is a dream since, really, where else but a dream would some horse need a Foley box, his uncle barks out, "Quag! Move! I need that box *now*!"

Claire turns, restless in the stall, and it's only then that Quag notices two little horse feet sticking out of her where you definitely would not want horse feet sticking out of you.

Oh, freak.

Freak. Freak. Freak.

"BOX!!" says his uncle.

Quag runs for the box. It has a duct tape label on it that says "Foaling Kit," which, along with the freaky baby horse feet sticking out of the horse's butt, explains a lot. He didn't even know Claire was pregnant. He just thought she was kind of a round-bellied sort of horse. By the time he wrestles the box down and gets back to the stall, Claire is down on her side, his uncle kneeling next to her.

Quag freezes in the door of the stall. There is stuff that looks like it should definitely be inside a horse hanging outside the horse along with the feet.

His uncle gestures impatiently for the box. Quag hands it over and then backs up against the wall, but uncle man isn't happy with that. "Look, kid," he says, "I don't know if this birds-and-bees stuff is a surprise to you or what, but the vet's out at Claridge's place, which is a good hour from here, and we don't have an hour. So I need your help." He waves a hand toward Claire's head stretched out on the straw. "You handle that end. I'll handle this end. Okay?"

Yeah. Deal.

But what's he even supposed to do?

"Get up there by her head. Keep her calm," says his uncle, who is wrapping Claire's tail in some sort of blue cloth stuff.

Quag gets down next to Claire's head in the straw. His hands are shaking. He doesn't know how to calm a horse and he doesn't know how to calm himself and he can feel the shakes moving down into his legs even though he's kneeling. Kneeling next to this huge animal laid out flat in the straw. Her body is also shaking, rhythmically shaking, like something huge and invisible is kicking her, and she's shuddering with the kicks.

His uncle pulls on what look like surgical gloves, but they go all the way up to his shoulders. Why would you need . . . ?

Oh.

Oh.

No, no, no.

"Quag." His uncle's voice is soft, but when Quag turns toward him, kneeling in the straw behind Claire, his eyes are focused on Quag's eyes, sharp and serious. "We're okay," his uncle says. "This is how it happens. This is how it happens every time. We're all okay."

How are they okay?

"Listen," says his uncle. "This is Claire's first foal, so she's more scared than you are."

Not possible.

Quag looks at Claire grunting in the straw, quaking under some invisible onslaught.

Okay, totally possible.

"This is what I want you to do," his uncle says. "You talk to her. Tell her what a pretty girl she is. Tell her she knows how to do this. Tell her we're going to take care of her. You got it?"

Quag looks down into Claire's brown eye. It feels like she can't see him at all. Like she is somewhere else. But she needs to be here.

"Quag," says his uncle. "You got it?" His voice is calm.

Quag grabs on to the calm of the voice. "Yeah," says Quag.

He looks down at Claire, and all he can think to do is press both hands gently against her sweat-flecked neck and rock back and forth with her as she shakes. Quag tells her everything his uncle told him to and more. He tells her it will be okay, it will be okay, you'll be okay. He tells her not to worry. He tells her he'll stay with her. He tells her he's scared too. That she is brave. That she will be a good mom. That she is strong. He's seen it. And, finally, he sings to her, low and quiet—a song his mom used to sing about hush-a-bye and all the pretty little horses.

And for a while, this is how it goes. Claire twitching and shaking. Quag whispering to her and stroking her neck. His uncle doing whatever he is doing back there, and Quag is not going to make the mistake of checking out what that is again.

Beside him, Claire suddenly rolls and surges to her feet. "Hold her," yells his uncle. Quag grabs the halter, but there is no holding a horse this big, and Claire drags him forward. A flurry of quiet swearing from uncle man, and then "Quag, I need you back here. Now!"

Quag stumbles back toward his uncle and there is blood in the straw, and Quag remembers a kid who fainted during a film in health class last year—how he had stood up at his desk and then gone down, like his bones had suddenly melted inside his skin. Quag wonders if this is how he felt before he dropped.

Because the horse feet have extended to become two bony legs and a baby horse face. The tongue is hanging out between the baby's lips, and it doesn't move at all. It looks dead. Is Claire's baby dead?

And then the little horse is sliding out, and Quag and his uncle both step forward and catch it as it falls. They both grunt and sink a little as the full weight hits their arms. And the baby is not dead at all, because it is thrashing around like anything. Uncle Jay is saying, "Easy. Easy, buddy," and they are lowering the baby horse down into the straw.

So. Turns out there is all kinds of freaky crap that comes out of a horse along with the baby. You don't even want to know. And some of that stuff is all over them, and Uncle Jay is peeling some of that stuff off the little horse and some of it is still hanging from Claire. But even with all that going on, Claire is turning around and sniffing at the little baby, who is sitting in the straw with his little neck stretched out and his little ears pointing straight up and his bony little legs folded under him. His hair is curly and wet. He's sitting there, big brown eyes looking all around him like he's trying to figure out where he is.

Quag feels a hand on his shoulder. "You did good," says Uncle Jay. "Real good." They stand together looking down at the little horse. Then, "Come on, let's give Claire some help." And Uncle

Jay tosses him a blue towel out of the bin and tells him to dry that baby off. Which, okay, Quag doesn't know how to do that, but he hasn't known how to do anything he's done so far tonight. So he scrubs the little horse down with the towel while Claire licks away at the baby's head. The baby seems to like it. And, watching this baby who's looking around, turning his funny ears this way and that, not afraid of him, not afraid of anything in this world, it feels to Quag like maybe he did do good.

Quag rubs his fingertips across the baby's coat. The baby has a funny, crooked stripe of white down his nose, but now that it's drying, the rest of his coat looks like it might be the same color as Claire's.

"Jay?"

"Yup."

"My mom's not visiting a friend, and she was way spun up the last time I saw her. She doesn't make good decisions when she's like that. We probably need to call your cop friend and find her."

His uncle looks at him. Now that he's paying attention, Quag can see that Jay's got bags under his eyes that are almost as big as Ollie's.

"I wondered," Jay says. "She used to get like that sometimes." He sighs and pulls his phone out of his pocket. "We're going to lose a little bit of control here, but you're right. I'll call," says Jay.

Quag hates to break it to him. They lost control a while ago.

BIRDS: THINGS NO ONE SEES

So in the spring, billions of birds fly north. No joke. Billions. There are so many that you can see them on weather radar. You can watch these massive bird clouds sort of throwing themselves into the air when they take off. But here's the thing—they fly at night, and they fly high. So people don't really know it's happening.

Because they can't see it.

So they don't care.

A million birds could be flying over their heads every night, but the night is dark, and people are asleep. So pretty much nobody even knows anything is going on.

TWENTY-SEVEN

Quag wakes up early, worried about his mom. But he knows where he is this time, and there's none of that weird breathing stuff going on, so he'll take it. He gets into some clothes and clatters down the stairs. Jay's sitting at the kitchen table going through a stack of mail under the warm glow of the red hanging lamp. He glances up as Quag comes in. He must see the question, even though Quag doesn't say it out loud. He shakes his head. "Haven't heard anything yet," he says.

Quag heads over to get some cereal out of the cupboard. "How's the baby horse?" Quag asks.

"Doing good. Doing real good," says Jay. "Trotting around like he owns the place."

Quag stares into the cupboard. They definitely need to get some better cereals in this house. Quag picks out the least old-man type.

"Hey," Jay says. "Go easy on Maggie today, okay?"

Quag turns toward him. Since when is Maggie someone who needs people to go easy on her?

Jay's doing pretty good at mind reading today. "Look," he says.

"Her family is in the process of losing their ranch this year. Most of the land's gone. The cattle got sold off last month, because the guy who bought the land runs a different breed. But someone's bought Maggie's mare, and they're coming for the horse today. I've given her extra work in the barn, so she won't have to be there when they come. But it's going to be a hard day. Go easy, all right?"

Quag eats his Cheerios. He's trying orange juice on them today, which is surprisingly not bad. What happens when you lose your ranch? Is it like being evicted from your apartment? "Will they have to leave?" he asks Jay.

Jay shrugs. "Depends. They kept the house. Her mom's worked part-time at the school for years to bring in a little money. Her dad's trying to find work."

"Okay," says Quag. But he's not exactly looking forward to heading out to the barn. He spends some time rinsing out his bowl and glass to put it off a little.

When he gets there, Maggie is standing outside of Claire's stall, looking at the new baby horse. "He's beautiful," she says, and he is beautiful, trotting around on his gangly legs exactly like he owns the place, but Quag can't help but think that it's a pretty sucky move by the universe to have a brand-new horse show up just in time to greet Maggie on the day she's losing her own horse.

Maggie doesn't seem any different than usual. Quieter, maybe. Okay, definitely quieter. There's no verbal poking at him today. There's no calling him "kid" like she's so much older than him that he's in some completely different category of people. No joking. No talking at all.

Just each of them going about their jobs. Feed the always-hungry calves. Gather the eggs. Change the dirty straw. Sweep the aisle. Same thing as always.

Until Maggie goes to scoop some sweet feed for Claire, and the lid of the bin they keep it in gets stuck. Like it does sometimes. And instead of just wiggling it—one side and then the other—like Maggie showed him how to do, suddenly Maggie is smashing her gloved fist down on it, and the cracked lid is hanging off to one side. She jams the scoop into the feed, and from where he's standing in the aisle, Quag can see that she's breathing hard. Halfway over to Claire's stall, Maggie makes an inarticulate sound and hurls the scoop down the aisle.

Sweet feed bounces everywhere. The metal scoop clangs against the leg of a trough. Mikey chicken and friends flap around in noisy alarm. Claire's head comes out of the stall opening, ears pricked and turned Maggie's way. Helga gives a disapproving moo, but then, opportunist that she is, loops her long pink tongue under the bars to pull in some of the pellets. Quag reaches over and slowly gets down the broom he just hung up and starts sweeping again.

"Did Jay tell you?" asks Maggie, hands on her knees and still breathing hard.

"Yeah," says Quag.

"Okay," says Maggie. "Okay." And when Quag bends to pick up the scoop, Maggie reaches for it. She digs out the sweet feed and dumps it in Claire's trough.

There are too many reminders here. Quag can see that now. While they're cleaning the room Jay uses for an office, there are pictures of horses on the wall and a horse calendar stuck to the metal filing cabinet and a horseshoe over the door. Then they're straightening up the tack room. This is not a good idea. Every single thing in here is a horse thing.

And when Maggie decides she's going to teach Quag how to clean a saddle, Quag knows it is a legit horrible idea. But he soaps up the saddle like she shows him and rinses it and rubs the conditioner into the leather with a soft rag. And if Maggie cries a little over the washing of the stirrup irons, Quag knows enough to know that a friend wouldn't make that awkward, so he doesn't.

When they finish, everything in the barn is looking good. Except Jay's desk, which Maggie studied for two seconds and decided against touching because "I am not in the mood to die in a paper avalanche today." Which makes Quag want to ask exactly when anyone would be in that particular mood, but he doesn't. Because he's going easy on Maggie today. Because, yeah, maybe even Maggie Loomis needs people to go easy on a day when life is hard.

Maggie stands back and looks over the tack room, everything soaped and oiled and buffed. "Let's go driving," she says, which surprises him after yesterday. He follows her out to her truck. "Uh-uh-uh," she says when she sees him heading toward the driver's side. "Passenger side, Mr. Let's-Drag-Race-Down-the-Lane." So he switches sides, and Maggie starts up the truck and texts Jay that they'll be gone for a while, and they're off. To drive through the middle of nowhere.

Maggie has the windows down and the music on, and it's not Quag's kind of music, but it's nice to have it on anyway. And Maggie knows better spots in the middle of nowhere than Quag's seen so far. She turns off the music and heads onto a gravel road that goes down between some hills, and, suddenly, they're in a place with lakes. Lakes and grass and, way off, even a few trees, but the water and grass are so beautiful, dancing together like they're both hearing the same song, that you don't even care about the trees. There's some bird with a strange beak that's almost as long as its whole body, wading along the shore poking at things. The wind brushes across the water making those ripply patterns it likes to make.

And when they come out from between a couple of lakes and there are big animals off in the grass, Quag only has to look for a second before he turns to Maggie. "Are those . . . ?" And she's nodding and grinning and turning the truck toward them, and Quag is driving past buffalo. In a pickup truck.

The heads on those things are way big—like massive—and all of them look like something from another time, or a wall in a cave, but they're just out here munching up grass—one of them tossing dust into the air with its hooves. Just because it wants to, maybe.

After they're past, Maggie pulls the truck over to the side and turns it off and hands the keys to Quag. "So now you're going to drive," she says. "And none of that Indy 500 stuff. You're just going to drive."

So he drives. And at first his back and neck are all tight, and he's just trying to keep everything on the road. But after a while it gets easier. Easier. Until he's driving, smooth and easy on this road that looks like it never ends, winding between the hills like it might never again bump up against a town or a train or anything but grass and water and wind.

AUDIO FILE ON QUAGMIRE TIARELLO'S MOM'S PHONE

Maggie Loomis driving her truck and singing "Wide Open Spaces." Loud and not exactly on key.

TWENTY-EIGHT

Maggie's feeding Claire peppermints when Quag comes into the barn the next morning. Quag wonders if he'll find a *Good Horse* container in the cupboard when he opens it. Maggie offers a peppermint to Quag.

"For me or for Claire?" Quag asks.

Maggie shrugs. "Whichever," she says.

But Quag doesn't want to stand around feeding Claire peppermints this morning. His mom's still missing, and, in spite of calling her in, no one seems to know a thing. Like she's just dropped off the earth. He needs to hear something. He needs to do something. Anything. Now. Even if it's scooping horse poop into a wheelbarrow.

There's the sound of a lawn mower starting up somewhere. No, scratch that. Because it's getting louder fast. Faster than a lawn mower travels. Maggie cocks her head like she's listening to it, and then her face breaks into a huge smile. "Come on," she says, trotting down the barn walkway. "Come on. Come on!" She's yelling over her shoulder and picking up speed.

People in cowboy boots. Ducks. Neither should run.

What is going on?

Quag follows Maggie out of the barn and down the lane. The noise of this motor is becoming a roar. A streak of red sweeps by, and something from the sky is landing on the lonely road out in front of the house.

What the heck?

Whatever this is—and if it was flying a minute ago, doesn't that mean it's some kind of plane?—it looks like a bobsled on wheels, if half the bobsled got chopped off and someone slapped a motor, a propeller, and an airplane tail on the back. And then, just for luck, this person added helicopter blades on top of the whole thing. No wings though. So how's that supposed to work? It's like the flying version of Ollie—all made out of parts—except this thing's not sad. It's amazing. All brilliant red metal and sleek curves and shiny motors.

The man in the front seat lifts off his helmet. It's the vet, Doc Hernandez, who had finally made it out here the night Claire had her baby. Which Quag should have known right off, because no two people in one county would have this kind of serious gray 'stache waxed out on the ends like that.

"How's your colt?" he asks Quag, like he's just pulled up in a pickup instead of dropping out of the sky in a souped-up flying sled.

"Good," Quag says.

Maggie's standing next to Quag, and she's grinning in a way he hasn't seen her grin before.

"Your uncle home?"

"Went into town," says Quag.

"That simplifies things," says the vet. He turns toward Maggie. "Heard about your mare," he says, and Quag sees the quick shine of tears fill Maggie's eyes. "I was out at Yung's, seeing to that bull of theirs, and I thought I'd come by on the way back, check on the colt, see if you wanted to take a spin. Get your mind off things."

Maggie's already reaching for the battered helmet he's holding out. "I have needed this all week," she says. She tugs on the helmet strap and climbs into the open cockpit behind the vet dude and buckles up. Quag gets the impression Maggie has done this before.

Then the engine is revving, and the helicopter blades are spinning, and they're speeding off down the deserted road. The airplane/hot rod/helicopter (what *is* this thing?) is lifting into the sky, throwing its shadow out to ripple across the grass below, and banking in a wide circle around the house and barn. Quag can see that Maggie has her arms spread out on either side in the air like she's a little kid. Like she has wings, and she's flying up there.

They ride around the rim of the world, Quag turning to follow the dash of red as they fly, and then they stitch trails across the blue dome of the sky for a while. When they touch down on the road in front of Quag, Maggie unbuckles her helmet and raises her arms to the sky. "That was so amazing!" she yells. She's smiling like she'll never stop. She vaults out of the cockpit, and then she's standing in front of Quag, holding out the helmet.

"Your turn," she says.

Really?

"What is this thing?" Quag asks her.

"Gyroplane," says Maggie, which doesn't help at all because Quag has never even heard of a gyroplane, and is he really going to get into this thing that looks like the tail is held on by two wires that could break at any minute and is flown by some dude who might be good at planes in addition to horses, but Quag's not really sure of that, and just because Maggie didn't die, doesn't mean that he won't. In fact, Maggie not dying seems like it makes it statistically more probable that he will, even though it doesn't really work like that. Also, he's never been in any kind of plane before, and he doesn't know how to do up the seat-belt-harness thing, and it looks seriously complicated.

But Maggie's holding out the helmet, and when she sees Quag hesitate, her smile gets even wider. Because Maggie hopped in like there was no reason in the world not to trust this wonky machine to take her up into the air. Is he really not going to take that helmet from her?

So he's climbing into the sleek seat with black chevrons stitched in red thread into the leather, and he's putting on the helmet, and Doc Hernandez is turning to explain the seat belt, which goes over both shoulders and clicks into a buckle in the middle. Quag pulls that seat-belt harness tight. And Quag watches every movement Doc makes with the controls as the gyroplane roars off down the road.

There is this moment as the wheels leave the ground when it feels like everything in Quag's chest lifts. The earth drops away. He is suspended in a blue arc. He's no longer thinking about Doc's hands on the controls. He sees only how the sunshine lights the

179

clouds scattered along the horizon, feels only the wind against his cheeks and chest and arms. There is nothing to watch over or manage or plan up here. There is only the world curving away on either side. And it is beautiful.

Do birds feel like this all the time? Does the wind going through their feathers feel like his T-shirt fabric beating against his skin? When they swoop low over the water, do they see the creek flashing under their wings like he's seeing it? Do they feel this free?

They finish the circle around the ranch, and now Quag sees that there is no rim—the grass goes on and on and on. They trace paths across the unending sky. And when they touch gently back down on the road, Quag sits for just a second with his eyes closed, seeing again the curve of the earth from above, following the meander of the bright creek.

Who can know if this is what a bird feels as it flies? Before today, Quag hadn't known to wonder. Before today he hadn't known that something like a gyroplane existed in the world. How many other things are out there that Quag doesn't even know about yet?

One thing he does know. From now on, during his whole life, whenever someone lands in front of him in a flying machine and there's an empty seat, Quag's climbing in.

AUDIO FILE ON QUAGMIRE TIARELLO'S MOM'S PHONE

A red gyroplane's engine and rotors.

TWENTY-NINE

The moon is different out here. Never chopped up, never behind trees, never in some place where you have to scoot around to get a look at it full. The light pours in Quag's bedroom window, and when he sits up in the thin-mattressed bed, all he can see out that window is that moon, so big it feels like he could climb out and maybe walk over to where it is almost resting on the horizon.

And then he becomes aware of the sound that had probably waked him—a faint, insistent dinging. He notices a shaft of light slanting across the sky down by that lonely mailbox. His eyes finally make sense of the shape he is seeing out there, and he's across the room, yanking open the door, pounding down the stairs, over the porch, and leaping onto the crackly, browning grass of the lawn.

He hears the screen door slam, and Uncle Jay comes scooting across the side porch and then onto the lawn, his undershirt white in the moonlight, and still trying to do up the pants he's thrown on. But Quag is running and past him, racing down the lane, soft dust spurting up around his bare feet. Running because he can see that the shape by the mailbox is a tipped car, slanted into the ditch that runs along the road, headlights pointed toward the sky. Even in the dark, Quag knows that car.

Rosie.

When he gets there, it looks like no one has been driving—the empty driver's seat angled there, silvered by the moon. But Quag knows that someone has been driving, and as he turns around, he sees her standing partway down the road in the middle, facing away from him. The moon shining on her hair makes it look white.

"Mom!"

She doesn't turn toward him. Doesn't seem to have heard him at all.

"Mom!" he yells again, starting toward her.

But there is something odd about her, something that makes him slow before he reaches her. She is brushing her hand through the air, like she's clearing spiderwebs from a path in front of her. But there are no webs.

"Mom?" He reaches out to touch her arm, and when she spins toward him, he can see that she is afraid of him. And then she's telling him that somebody took her son, she needs her son, they took him, where is her son? And Quag is trying to say, "I'm right here. Mom! I'm right here."

But she doesn't know him. He can see it in her eyes that she doesn't know him. That she's terrified. That maybe she thinks he took her son.

A pair of run-down cowboy boots crunch up to stand next to Quag. Quag's mom backs away.

"Is she like this often?" asks Uncle Jay, quietly.

"No," says Quag.

"No." Uncle Jay says it flat, like he's not questioning Quag, not calling him a liar, just considering the meaning of that word. And Quag remembers the night in the barn when the colt was born, how afterward, when everything was almost over and Jay was just washing Claire down with a sponge, Claire had turned and rested her big head on Jay's shoulder, and Jay had paused in what he was doing and stood, leaning his head against Claire's.

The moon brushes silver over everything out here on the road, like somehow that's going to help, but it seems like the wrong color for anything that's happening here. Quag looks at his mom, who has lost her son, standing in the moonlight pushing away things that he can't see.

"Almost never," Quag says. Because that's the real answer. And because sometimes you have to take a chance.

Uncle Jay sighs. "Kid, we're going to need some help here," he says, and he fishes his phone out of his pocket.

They have followed the ambulance. They have filled out the forms, what they could of them anyway. They've been told to go home. That there's nothing they can do right now. The nurse will call and let them know when his mom can have visitors.

But Quag isn't ready to go. "I want to see my mom," he says to Jay, after the nurse heads off to handle someone else.

So now, they haven't exactly sneaked in, because apparently you can't really sneak in to this floor, but they have gone out and come in a different entrance and gotten to the floor where Jay thinks his mom is. Uncle Jay is trying to get information from a different nurse. She is, Jay says, someone he knows. As far as Quag can tell, that isn't helping at all. She's standing behind the counter at the nurses' station, and her short gray Afro and raised eyebrows are adding up to a no-nonsense, don't-waste-my-time kind of look.

"Who is he?" The nurse jerks her thumb in Quag's direction.

It's four a.m. Quag is in the middle of a white box of a hospital trying to find a mom who doesn't know him anymore. The question seems weighted, dangerous.

Who is he?

He is someone who has raced the sun across seven states in a car named Rosie. He is someone who gets up every Saturday and logs into his mom's bank account and pays the bills, so they'll get paid. He is someone who can make Cassie Byzinski smile when she hadn't planned on smiling. He's someone who has helped a baby horse be born. He is someone who might be starting to be friends with Maggie Loomis. He is someone who has waged war with every stupid teacher, every jerk kid, and every inane assignment since he was seven, just to have something solid to fight against while this shadowy thing he couldn't fight loomed in the corners of his apartment, pushed against the edges of his mom's mind. He is someone who for fourteen years has kept his mom safe and then couldn't keep her safe anymore.

"He's her son," says Uncle Jay, leaning his arms on top of the high counter in front of the nurses' station. "When will we be able see her?"

But the nurse is asking the questions here. "How old is he?" she demands.

"What is your problem, Danisha?" says Uncle Jay. "A kid needs to see his mom."

"It's a locked unit, Jay. There are rules."

"He's twenty-three."

The nurse gives Uncle Jay a look.

"He's twenty-three. Write it on your friggin' forms."

The nurse's look has turned glacial.

"He doesn't need to be twenty-three, Jay. He does need to wait until she's stable. He does need to come during visiting hours. And I was asking because we have support groups, not because I'm trying to deny him entry. So you can come down from that high, high horse of yours and stop being the cantankerous old fart that you are."

That went well.

The nurse's face softens. She turns toward Quag. "I'm Danisha Johnson," she says. She hands him a card. "This is going to be the number you call when you want information about your mom, okay?"

"Yeah," says Quag. "Okay."

He and Uncle Jay both stare at this little card like maybe it's going to tell them what to do next. It doesn't.

"May as well head back, kid," Uncle Jay says. "Can't do anything here that we can't do from there. And the food is better there."

Quag gives him props for trying to bring some humor into this, but Quag is not in the mood. He follows Uncle Jay's cowboy-boot shuffle down the ugly white hallway full of ugly white tiles and ugly white lights and people in ugly green scrubs. The box of the elevator sighs down through the floors and opens them out in the emergency room where they came in, and everything is the same as it was. There's the receptionist with the long lavender nails, tapping her fingers on her keyboard. There's the guy holding his arm and rocking. There's the lady with the kids, still fighting over the markers. There's the ambulance driver standing outside the doors having a smoke.

And nobody cares. Which is a big surprise, right?

They head out the doors and find the old truck in the visitors' lot and pull out onto the highway. It's coming on morning, but the light is cold. The road stretches out blank in front of them all the way to the horizon, and there's just the growl of the engine and the silence of a day gone wrong. They ride like that past mile marker after mile marker, past barbed-wire fences, past black cows with white faces.

They drive west as the sun rises in the east, as if they are running from everything bright in the world. As if they can't bear to see what the light will uncover. But in the end, the light always catches up with you. No matter how fast you go. No matter how long you've been running.

People see his mom as a disaster, he knows they do. He's seen how the other parents at orientation make sure they don't sit by her, avoiding her tentative hello as they slide their sleek selves past this woman with the hair that needs a touch-up.

And some days maybe she is a disaster.

But other days, she is so alive. That's what he wants to tell everyone. He wants to tell them about the time she woke him up at 4:30 in the morning because "Quag, you have never lived until you've seen the sun come up from a rooftop. Get up. Open the window. I've got blankets and orange rolls and coffee." And they had watched, quiet together, and it had been the most beautiful thing.

She's funny. Saying stuff under her breath when she's supposed to be serious. Doing sharp, running commentary as she drives around town that makes Quag grin.

She's infuriating. All the things she misses, all the things she can't do that moms are supposed to do—pay the bills, sign the papers, take you to the stupid dentist, show up when she's supposed to show up. So you end up walking home during a blizzard in your gym shorts and a T-shirt with everyone looking at you as they drive past.

She tries. People say that like it's nothing. "She tries." But it is everything. She tries so hard—keeps getting up and going to work every morning, keeps finding a new job when she loses one to a spin, keeps starting over, keeps trying to find a way.

We all have ways of living in the world. We all have brains wired into our bodies, brains that send the bright thoughts winking through the latticework in our skulls. His mom's brain just happens to be this wild roller coaster, this swerving-car-along-the-edge-of-a-ravine-type brain, and even though that sometimes means she's driving with one wheel over the edge, maybe it also means that sometimes she's flying.

Maybe she loves flying.

Maybe when she's revving high, it feels like that moment when you leave the ground in a gyroplane and the world drops away and you're not tied to anything at all and you're free. She always says, "Don't look back," and Quag never even knows what that's supposed to mean, but maybe it means she just feels the wind in her hair and sees how blue the sky is as she soars through the air in this beautiful arc. Free.

Maybe it means she never even notices how fast the ground is coming up to meet her.

THIRTY

The closer they get to the ranch, the more jittery Quag starts to feel. Like there is a well full of things that he has always kept a tight cover on, but now someone has cracked that cover, maybe even lost it, and things are spilling out. Mom lost, alone in a house, alone by a road, not seeing Cassie again, no way home, looks from a stranger, the way the ambulance guy held his mom down—everything is down in that dark well, and now those things are climbing up the sides, crawling fast.

Jay isn't saying anything, hasn't said anything since back at the hospital when they got in the truck, and that helps. Because Quag is busy right now. He closes his eyes and concentrates on throwing each thing back down as it comes over the lip of the well. But there are so many things climbing.

Uncle man doesn't say a word until they come in through the screen porch and they're in the hall leading to the kitchen. He clears his throat. "Okay," he says. "School starts end of August. We might need to think about getting you registered here in . . ."

Quag has stopped in the hall and is looking at him. The sudden anger that is billowing up in Quag feels enormous. Unending.

Like it's tumbling out of that same deep well, blowing all of the smaller things out of the way as it comes. It's rolling up to swirl around his heart and surge into his lungs and wrap around his brain, and then, still unfolding, like one of those ash clouds that sweeps down from the banks of a volcano, tumbling cars and houses in front of it until its blackness swallows everything.

How dare he. How dare Jay assume. How dare he decide without asking. How dare he talk about this on a day when Quag needs every scrap of concentration just to hold himself together.

The black cloud surges all the way to his fingertips and the ends of each strand of his hair, until it fills him, and Quag shatters, shards of obsidian raining down around him in the hall, and he is roaring and pounding the wall, his fist thudding into the plaster over and over and over. Red streaks of pain shoot through the darkness. And then Jay is reaching through the smoke and the rubble and the fear and holding both of Quag's arms so he can't swing. Quag can feel his uncle's sinewy arms looped through his elbows and his uncle's steady heart beating through his back.

"I know, kid, I know," says Uncle Jay, and maybe he does, but Quag doesn't want to hear it. He shrugs out of Jay's arms and runs. Runs across the flat crunch of the yard grass, across the lane. Runs until he pushes through the door of the barn. Into the warm, hay-scented barn with dust floating lazily through the air, the sweet smell of calf feed floating past, the sour of cow piss, the fragrant dustiness of Claire and her baby, the rasp of Helga's tongue as she slowly, endlessly carves out the center of her salt block. Beyond the walls, Quag can feel the grass and the gold eyes of the sandhill crane and the rain when it sweeps down like a silver curtain.

But it isn't what he wants.

It isn't a cool rooftop in summer with the smell of pizza drifting over from Snarkey's. It isn't his mom slamming around in the next room making a royal mess because she's decided to make something she saw on a cooking show that takes thirteen pans and a blowtorch. It isn't a soundboard with green lights. It isn't Cassie reaching over to share a new package of pretzel nibs.

It isn't any of those things, and the loss hollows out Quag's bones and drops him down in the dirt. He hears a roaring in his ears, but the roaring is him. He lets the roar echo around the rafters of the old barn, howling out all the bitter tears that he hasn't let himself cry since he was eleven and first realized that his mom would never get better.

When he calms down, he feels Claire lipping at his hair, and somehow that makes him cry again, but it's a short cry this time, and part of the time he's laughing a little, because when he rolls over, Claire does one of those loose-lipped horse snorts all over him. And even though it smells like hay and is a little wetter than you actually want, somehow it makes things better.

His hand hurts. When he reaches down to it, he can feel sticky blood, so he doesn't look at it. He's so tired. He's so tired that he's just going to close his eyes and stay here, maybe forever, curled up on the floor outside the horse stall.

There's a creak of the barn door. Square-toed, run-down cowboy boots in front of his tired eyes. Other boots next to them tooled with a red rooster. Uncle Jay is down on his knees and sliding his arms under Quag's shoulders and lifting him into a sitting position, and Doc is gently picking up Quag's hand, which makes Quag pull in the air sharp between his teeth. "Next time you want to punch something, young man, choose something that's not a wall," the vet says.

"He doesn't need a lecture from you, Diego," says Uncle Jay. "You've punched a wall or two in your lifetime. Don't make me remind you of the times."

So that shuts Doc up, and he sprays Quag's hand with something cold that hurts like all get-out for a minute but makes the hand hurt less after. He wraps it up snug and says, "It's broken, so you'll need to take him in anyway, but that'll keep him for the moment."

Uncle Jay helps Quag to his feet. They walk to the pickup and start the long drive to the hospital for the second time that day.

"Let's try this again," says Uncle Jay as he parks his pickup next to Maggie's in the lane when they finally get back home. Quag has a new green cast from mid-palm up to his elbow. "And please don't hit anything this time. I'm too tired to do that drive again."

They're both too tired to do that drive.

"Listen," says Jay. "I was just trying to say that staying here is an option. That you're welcome here." Jay turns toward him and looks at Quag with his sad-dog eyes. "It shouldn't be all on you to take care of your mom."

Oh yeah? He's always taken care of his mom. Always. Who is

going to take care of his mom if he doesn't?

"You're fourteen," says Jay. "You've got other things you'll be wanting to do while you're fourteen."

Quag tries to wrap his head around what Jay is saying, but he's so tired. Everything seems to float off as soon as he tries to think it. Except for one thing. He's always taken care of his mom, but it's not working now.

He's out of plans.

BIRDS: COWBIRDS

They lay their eggs in other birds' nests. And then they head off to do who knows what. But the thing is that a cowbird chick hatches faster than almost any of the other birds do. And then half the time, the cowbird chick kicks the other eggs or babies clear out of the nest. Takes over. Or if it doesn't, it grows so much bigger, so much faster, that it can stretch its huge mouth up higher than any of the other babies. So it gets way more than its share of the food.

The chick gets bigger and bigger and bigger, until maybe the bird that's trying to take care of it is only half its size. So now that bird that keeps bringing the food has this huge, hungry, too big thing that has taken over its whole life.

Does that bird know what's happening? Or does it just think this is how life is, this huge open mouth stretching eternally up to meet it?

THIRTY-ONE

Quag has his phone back. They rescued it from the wreck in the ditch before it was towed off. Quag pulled the two bucks and the debit card that he'd hidden in the glove compartment out too, so at least he has a little money now.

When his phone powers up, there are texts from a bunch of different people. Jax from a week and a half ago with an idea for another sound file they might need. Rhia from the morning after he left saying to hurry up with the doughnuts already. Mikey, a day later, wanting to know if he's mad at them or something. Yesterday, Jake texted saying he's back from band camp, and he wants to know where Quag is. Mac has sent him a video of a whole bunch of parrots, impossibly green, chilling together in a tree.

Cassie. There is a string of texts from Cassie following him all the way across the US. Cassie is furious.

Quag doesn't know what to say to any of them.

Maggie's been pretty dialed down the last two days since Quag and Jay got back from the hospital. Going easy on Quag. But she is in a majorly good mood this evening as they finish up. Like she's doing this weird kind of cowboy-dance thing down the center of the barn aisle while she's sweeping. When Jay comes in the door, she lets out a whoop and follows him toward the office.

What's up with Maggie?

There's the sound of voices back and forth, some laughter. Maggie comes out of the office a minute later, fanning a stack of twenties and making little kissy noises toward the bills.

Seriously?

"Quag!" Jay calls from the office. "You got a minute?"

Quag comes to the door, and Jay reaches a stack of bills toward him. "Payday," he says. "Two weeks' worth."

Jay is paying him?

Jay is getting freaky good at this reading-your-mind thing he does, because he says, "What? Did you think I was asking you to do all this for nothing?"

"Pretty much." If he's going to know what you're thinking anyway, you might as well say it out loud.

"Nah," Jay says, turning back toward the desk. "It's hard work, you're a hard worker, and I appreciate the help. It's let me get to some things I haven't been able to get to for a while."

That part's a lie. Quag happens to know that Maggie has been doing all the barn work since school let out without any help from Jay. So it's not like Quag freed up any time. Jay's just paying double for what gets done now. Assuming he paid Quag as much as he paid Maggie.

How much did he pay Maggie?

Still. Quag's not going to argue with him. The bills feel good in his hand, and at least the top one is a twenty, and he wants to go outside and count over what he's got. But he just folds the money in half and puts it in his pocket where a wallet would go if he hadn't left his wallet back home on his dresser in New York. How much does he have now with this plus the money and debit card from the car?

"Thanks," Quag says.

"You bet," says Jay, and he's already digging into a file folder on the desk and is on to something else.

But Maggie is at the door to the office. "Let's go, kid," she says. "Can I take him to Charney's?" she asks Jay.

"Sure," says Jay. Like Quag is just going to follow Maggie wherever she is currently headed.

"Come on, come on," says Maggie, putting a hand on Quag's back and steering him out the door. And the weird thing is that Quag lets himself be steered. Because sometimes when you follow Maggie, you get to drive a truck between hills with buffalo hanging out on them, and sometimes when you follow Maggie, a gyroplane drops out of the sky. Who knows what could happen on the way to Charney's? Whatever Charney's is.

It's not a red gyroplane. And she doesn't let him drive. But Charney's turns out to be okay. Because the milkshakes are epic. They're so thick that the lady at the counter turns each one upside down for a second before she hands it to you, just to show off.

"My treat," says Maggie. "Because I just got a raise due to me taking on managerial duties over your sorry butt." So Maggie did get paid more than him.

There's a shake called the Whoa Cowboy that has every single mix-in on the menu in it. "I got that once," says Maggie. "It was pretty random. But everything else is good. Jay likes the mint-with-cookies one." Maggie orders the Banana Split in a Cup, and Quag orders the All the Candy Bars Ever shake, and it might really have all the candy bars ever in it. It's that thick.

"Man, I love payday," says Maggie. "We are not going to need dinner tonight."

Quag will take it. Everything's all messed up with his mom. She's still in the hospital, and he hasn't even been allowed to see her yet. All the candy bars in the world aren't going to fix anything.

But they don't hurt either.

Maggie puts her feet up on the chair beside her and looks out the front window at the late summer sunlight as she eats. There's a dinosaur made out of rusty car parts in front of the shop. He's holding an ice-cream cone in his little metal claw.

"I always feel bad for that T. rex," says Maggie. "I don't think he can reach his mouth."

Quag looks out the window, considering. She's right. Those little arms aren't going to do it. "He could toss it," says Quag. "Toss and catch."

But Maggie is shaking her head. "No arm strength," she says, like she's already thought this through. "And he'd have to get it up and around that big jaw. What are the odds?" She takes another scoop of her shake, still looking out at the T. rex. "Nope," she says. "Some things just aren't happening." And Quag, looking out at a dinosaur who isn't even alive, feels a deep sadness spread through him over the impossibility of that cone ever getting into that mouth.

THIRTY-TWO

"Ready?" asks Jay.

Quag's not ready. He wishes Ollie was in his usual place in the middle of the truck, so that Ollie could lay his heavy head on Quag's leg and Quag could rub his soft, soft ears. But they couldn't bring him. They're sitting in the parking lot of the hospital. They're going to visit his mom.

"Yep," Quag says.

But Jay is drumming his fingers on the big steering wheel. "Okay. Give me a minute," he says. So he isn't ready either. Quag stares out the window at the yellow car with the dented fender parked next to them. A doll with pale purple hair on one side and what looks like a homemade haircut on the other is tipped halfway over in the back seat next to a Subway bag.

Jay is bouncing the heels of his boots on the floor of the truck. He's dressed about the same as he is any other day—jeans and a plaid shirt—but Quag noticed that his boots were cleaned and oiled up this morning when he climbed in the truck. Which might be the equivalent of dressing up.

"Okay," Jay says, rolling his shoulders. "Okay, I'm good." He opens the door and climbs down from the truck. When he walks across the parking lot beside Quag, he walks like he's not nervous at all—just his usual cowboy shuffle.

Maybe everyone in the world is scared of something. Maybe everyone in the world is pretending they're not. Right now, Quag is scared that when he sees his mom, who hadn't known who he was last time he saw her, things will be different between them. That she'll be different. Not his mom, somehow.

He's also scared that she'll be able to tell that Quag is so mad at her. He wasn't mad until she was found. Just scared. But now that she's found, he's furious. She ran out on him. She left him by the side of a stinking road. She did that. It was only a fluke that he found Uncle Jay. Don't care how spun up you are, you don't leave your own kid on the side of the road. There is no excuse for that. So maybe he's afraid that things won't be the same because he's not the same.

They go in a different door than they went in last time. His mom's been moved to another floor. This part of the hospital is nicer. Big windows. A cart where you can buy snacks or cards. Couches and armchairs grouped around this fake fireplace. Like people would be sitting around in a hospital just chatting it up. Reading a book. Something.

But it gets hospital-y as soon as they step into the elevator. A dude with a walker and a kind of metal coatrack thing on wheels—except it's got a plastic bag of who knows what that's being piped into the guy's arm—asks them which floor they're headed to. A woman with a tired face leans her head against the back wall of the elevator and closes her eyes like she might fall asleep right here between floors.

When they get to the floor his mom's on, Quag lets Jay do all the talking to the nurse behind the counter in the hall. Quag is going into that part of his head he escapes to when a teacher is droning on and on—the not-dealing-with-this part. He'll have other things to deal with soon enough.

They walk down the hall and are buzzed through a door. They're in an area with too many lights, too few doors. The nurse leads them past a few rooms with beds to another room with a jigsaw puzzle set out on a table. His mom is sitting on a beige plastic couch to the side of all this, looking small.

She looks up and sees Quag and then looks down again. Like she's embarrassed. Like maybe she's thinking about what happened at the side of that road too. But she knows him this time. He can tell.

Uncle Jay has stopped in the doorway. His mom is twisting the hem of the T-shirt she's wearing between her fingers and not looking at either of them. Really? They're both going to leave this up to him?

Perfect. Couldn't be better. Quag is tired, tired, tired of everyone leaving everything up to him.

And then his mom, still looking down, reaches out her hand and pats the seat next to her. Quag moves to sit. His tennis shoes are dusty from all the barn work. They almost don't look blue anymore.

His mom reaches out her hand, picks up Quag's hand that isn't in the cast, and, in a swift movement, pulls it up and kisses the back of it. And Quag wants to ask, "Why?" and "Did you know what you were doing when you drove away?" "Did you even think about me during those days you were missing?" "Do you mean what you say out loud when you're in a bad spin?" But he doesn't say any of those things. Just pulls his hand back from her and tucks it under his leg.

He does not want to be doing this here in front of the woman in a baggy sweatshirt staring at them as she drifts by in the hall, here in this place where he can hear a man yelling wordlessly every few seconds like he's on a timer. And, sorry: A kiss on the back of the hand isn't going to do it.

Nope.

"Moira?" comes Jay's voice. Quag can see the square-toed boots in front of them and Jay scuffing at the linoleum with the toe of one.

A pause. Then "Jay Jay?" and Quag's mom is on her feet, and she and Jay are holding on to each other and rocking back and forth, back and forth, and Jay is saying, "It's okay. It's going to be okay. We got this. We're going to be okay." And Quag can tell from their voices that both of them are crying. Uncle Jay reaches out his barn-rough hand toward Quag.

But Quag leaves him hanging. It's too much. He can't think how they're supposed to start making any of this right.

AUDIO FILE ON QUAGMIRE TIARELLO'S PHONE

Ollie wheezing and snuffling in his sleep.

THIRTY-THREE

The number on Quag's phone comes up as No Caller ID.

Probably Nurse Johnson trying to talk him into one of her support groups again. Quag almost doesn't answer. But she'll just call back. Or call Uncle Jay. She's stubborn like that. She's trying to wear him down.

He picks up.

"Hey," says a voice.

It's not Nurse Johnson. It's his mom.

He thought she was only supposed to call during the afternoons.

"Hey, Mom."

"I'm getting out of here," she says.

"Not for a while, Mom. They've got to work through the medications. See what works. It takes a while."

"I'm getting out," she repeats. "Louie says they can't keep me. Not over seventy-two hours. I'm signing out."

Who is Louie?

"Come get me," she says. "We're heading out."

Quag looks up at the ceiling. There's a crack running through the plaster at a slant.

Could they just head out?

Could they go back home? Could he walk back into ArtCamp one morning? Tell everyone that they'd had to go out of town unexpectedly? Funeral, maybe. People don't like to push you about stuff like funerals. And he could say his phone died, and he forgot his charger, and his mom said she wasn't buying another one when he had two perfectly good chargers sitting on his dresser at home. So, sorry he didn't get the audio files to them before the phone died, but you know moms.

Could they go home? And catch up on the rent and live in the town by the lake with all the green trees and a pizza place next door and actual sidewalks that would take you down to an actual park where there's a duck that loves peanut butter?

Could they? Could he walk over to the house with the wide porch and the baskets of red flowers and knock on the door? Would Cassie open that door? Could that happen?

He could bluff big. He could make it stick.

"I'm getting out of here," says his mom. "I'll be out front, waiting. You got it?"

"Got it," says Quag.

Quag takes one credit card from the wallet on top of the refrigerator. He takes the keys and hopes that Jay's truck works pretty much like Maggie's does. He waits till Jay goes out to the barn to fix the float on Helga's watering trough. Then he gets in the truck and drives.

THIRTY-FOUR

When Quag walks into the ranch house kitchen a couple of hours later, both Jay and Maggie are sitting at the old oak table, and Quag instantly feels their eyes on him. They have definitely noticed that Quag's come into the room. Jay lets out a shaky sigh, like he's been holding his breath for a while, and drops his head into his hands for a second. Maggie picks up a dish towel sitting on the table and chucks it at Quag.

Quag sidesteps.

He tosses Jay's credit card onto the table. "I filled up the truck," Quag says. "It was below a quarter tank." He sets the grocery bags he's carrying down on the counter. "Also, if I'm going to stay here, I'm taking over cooking dinner."

"Can you cook?" asks Maggie.

"Can Jay cook?" says Quag.

"Good point," says Maggie.

"Hey!" says Jay.

"Heating up chili in a microwave is not cooking," Maggie says.

Quag unloads the groceries. Five cartons of ice cream, and all of them good flavors. Hamburger patties, buns, dill pickles, cheese slices. A jar of extra-chunky peanut butter, red pepper flakes, bread. Pop-Tarts, Cocoa Pebbles, Cinnamon Toast Crunch, a family pack of mac and cheese, chips, pudding cups, and a box of frozen sausage biscuit sandwiches. That was as much as he'd been able to buy with the money Jay had given him on payday.

"I see you're continuing the no-vegetables diet," says Maggie.

"There's mint in one of the ice creams," observes Jay. "Mint is a plant."

"Pickles are vegetables," says Quag.

"You're both going to get scurvy," says Maggie.

"All right," says Jay, laying one hand over the credit card on the table and holding out his other hand toward the truck keys hanging from Quag's pocket, which Quag gives him. "We need to come to an understanding about who owns this credit card and these keys. But I'm glad you're back home."

Home doesn't feel exactly like the right word to Quag. But he lets it stand. Close enough for now.

THIRTY-FIVE

"Hey," says Jay.

Quag looks up from the book he'd pulled out of the old bookcase in the hall.

Jay's standing in the hallway outside of Quag's bedroom. "I checked in with the hospital. Your mom is still there. They're aware of the situation. They're working through it."

Jay steps into the doorway, leans against the frame. "I really thought you had run," Jay says.

Yeah, well. Quag thought he had run too.

But then he had been trying to drive that truck (which was not as easy as Maggie's) through town on the way to the road that leads to the bigger city where the hospital is, and he had driven past Charney's. And there was that rusty T. rex, standing out front, still holding an ice-cream cone that he was never, never, never going to be able to reach. And Quag had thought, *Nope.*

Because how is anything ever going to change? It's never going to change. He's always trying to keep things under control—working to head things off, to manage things, but it never works for long. It's the same thing over and over. How is he going to stop losing everything—apartments, places, people, friends—every time his mom hits a big spin that slams apart the pieces he's pulled together? How are they ever going to be okay?

He wants something to last. He wants something he can keep. He doesn't know if he can find that here. He really doesn't. Everything about this ranch in Nebraska feels strange. Not like his world. But it's the first place where someone is trying to help. It's the first place where they have someone else who cares. It's the first place where maybe something *could* change.

So don't they have to try it?

He has to try it.

And he'd turned the truck around and driven back to the ranch.

Jay shuffles his boots on the floor and softly thumps his fist a couple of times on the doorjamb. "I'm glad you didn't run," he says.

And Quag can't really think of what to say to that. It feels like something big, like something you might need to say the right words about. He searches around for how he feels about any of this, but everything's so mixed up right now. The closest he can get is that it doesn't feel bad to be here. That it feels okay.

"What are you reading?" asks Jay. Quag holds up the book. "Ah, good old Louis L'Amour," says Jay.

This is the third one Quag has read. The bookcase is packed with these cowboy books, all written by this same guy, and Quag has a question. "Are all these pretty much the same story with slightly different characters?" he asks Jay.

"Yeah, pretty much," says Jay.

"Then why bother?"

Jay looks up at the ceiling like he's considering. Then he shrugs. "Sometimes you just want a story where the good guy wins."

THIRTY-SIX

Maggie has a bunch to say today. Because earlier this morning, Maggie saw the picture of Cassie on Quag's lock screen. He'd put it there while his mom was driving across the world, because who's going to see your lock screen while you're stuck in a car to nowhere? But then he forgot to take it off. So Maggie's been giving Quag grief all afternoon. They're sitting in the bed of her pickup, taking a break, and Maggie's at it again. "Lock-screen photo," she says. "Spill."

"Your truck got a name?" asks Quag.

"Can't name trucks. Like naming cows. If you name it, you're twice as sad when it dies."

"So you just call it Truck?"

"Stop trying to change the subject, Quag. Who's the photo on your lock screen?"

"So, here's a game," says Quag. "You take the title of a movie. Then by changing only one word in the title, you have to change the movie from a comedy to a tragedy, or a tragedy to a comedy."

Maggie pops some of her cinnamon gum in and offers Quag a piece, which he takes. Maggie always adds in a new piece of gum as soon as the flavor's running out on the old piece, so by this time of day she has a serious wad in there. "I don't get it," she says, tucking the gum in her cheek. "Give an example." She stretches her boots out in front of her. "Also, I see what you did right there, Tiarello. And we will circle back to the mysterious lock-screen photo when I'm bored again, but let's go with this game of yours for now."

They play for a while. Maggie's good at the game. Maybe even better than Mikey. When they run out of steam, Maggie unwraps another piece of gum. "So, does she know she's your lock-screen photo?" she asks.

Maggie equals relentless.

"No," says Quag. "She doesn't."

Low whistle from Maggie. "Kid, that is a total newbie mistake. Better let her know about that." Maggie stretches her arms and leans her head back against the cab window. They sit looking off across the low hills for a bit. "How you doing with all this stuff with your mom?" she finally asks. "You gonna be okay?"

Quag lets the question sit for a minute. "Yeah," he says. "I think so. Eventually." Because that's the real answer. That's the answer you would give a friend. "How you doing with that thing with your ranch?" he asks.

Maggie blows out a long breath. "You know what I hate most about all that? It feels like I'm losing my dad at the same time that we're losing everything else. He doesn't know anything but the ranch. Like he never even flipped burgers in town during the summer when he was in high school or anything. It's always been the ranch his whole life. He's looking for work, but he hasn't really found anything. He's almost not who he was anymore, he's so shut down." Maggie sighs. "You and me, kid, we are having fairly sucky years this year."

That's the truth.

They sit listening to the wind whisper through the grass for a while. Then Maggie stretches and gets to her feet. "Break's over," she says. "Let's roll."

"You do realize that we're doing the exact same thing every single day, right?" says Quag. "There's got to be a better way to do this."

"Yeah?" says Maggie. "Well, when you figure that one out, smart boy, you just let me know. You put an animal in a pen, you're immediately responsible for whatever that animal needs. And that includes clearing out muck." She hops down from the tailgate of her truck, and Quag follows her.

Which is a habit he's really going to have to break one of these days.

Quag wants to use the credit card again, but he asks this time. Once Jay understands what he's up to, he agrees. Quag hands over the last twenty he's got. Cassie's twenty. And then he DoorDashes four glazed doughnuts to ArtCamp. Because glazed are the best. But he also sends a couple of ones with sprinkles, a couple of powdered, and three of the ones with the crunchy cinnamon stuff on top and the little apple pieces in them. He even throws in a coconut one. Because you never know, maybe Mikey likes that kind.

AUDIO FILES ON QUAGMIRE TIARELLO'S PHONE

Wind blowing through the grass.
A little colt, whinnying.
The chittering of a sandhill crane.

THIRTY-SEVEN

Quag's been climbing up the derrick a lot lately. It's a mega tall tower jutting out of the middle of one of the pastures, and it's a good place to think. Quag climbs up today. Which isn't as easy as you'd think with a cast. Up past the first platform, which is tall enough if you just want to sit and think and watch the wind roll over the grass, but isn't tall enough today. Up past the missing rung, which is where he starts to feel a shake in his soul if he looks down. Up until he comes out on the tiny platform at the top where the big windmill paddles spin over him with slow, creaking majesty, and he can feel their power as it passes through his chest and spine and legs, as if the machine has claimed him, knitting him neatly into its being.

Quag stands and feels the huge power of the wind and the steel and the water being pulled up from deep layers underground for the cows. He sees the cows, spread out like black stones tossed into the sea of rolling grass. He sees the house on its raft of lawn, the old blue pickup tethered to it.

He follows the road with his eyes until it disappears, and then he imagines lifting off and flying over it to where it runs through

a little town with a big church and an ice-cream shop with a dinosaur out front. Back to the interstate he'd fly, skimming along
above the four lanes. He'd swoop down to look at a yellow purse
sitting by the side of the road and skim over the green oasis around
the river, brushing the tips of the tall grass as he flies, just to see
the birds rise up around him. He'd fly faster and faster, past a pink
diner in Iowa, past Conneaut and Erie and the wide lake, and over
the green trees of New York State until he'd arrive at a long lake
with a little town spread out like a fan on the north shore. And he
would set himself gently down on the sidewalk in front of Cassie's
house.

Cassie would be sitting on the porch steps, the wind riffling
her short, dark hair, and she'd stand and walk toward him like
she'd been waiting for him. She'd stop in front of him.

And he'd say, "I'm not coming back."

"I hate that," Cassie would say.

"Me too."

Cassie would look off toward the lake. "Quag?"

"Yeah?"

"Let's pretend for a while that this isn't happening."

"Okay."

"I was just going to take a walk," Cassie would say. "Along that
path behind the hardware store. The one by the creek. Want to
come?"

"Sure."

"There's all kinds of birds down there." And Cassie would grin
at him. "That trail is full of birds."

"Right." He'd smile down at her. "Birds. Perfect. Couldn't be better."

They'd walk along the creek, under the green leaves of the birches. They'd stand elbow to elbow on the old stone bridge and watch the blossoms from a redbud float past. They'd walk back to Cassie's house and sit on the porch steps until Aunt Becca called Cassie in. By the time Quag got back to the derrick, the sun would have set.

The lights from the ranch house windows shine in the dark. A door creaks open, throwing a long slant of white across the dark ground. "Quag?" Uncle Jay shouts out into the night. "Time to come in."

And Quag starts climbing down.

When he gets back inside, Uncle Jay is sitting at the kitchen table with a set of reading glasses on that Quag has not seen before and a pile of books. It's a big pile—looks like he checked out every book the library had on this subject. The one in his hands is bright green with a big magenta heart on it and the title *When Someone You Love Lives with Mental Illness* splashed across the cover. He glances up over the top of the black half-glasses as Quag comes into the room.

"Think that's gonna help?" asks Quag, nodding at the book. He scoots the stuff in the fridge around until he finds the cans of Dr Pepper that he knows Uncle Jay will have hidden in there.

"Can't hurt," says Uncle Jay, and goes back to his book.

Quag finds a Snack Pack with three chocolate puddings left

and balances the puddings and the soda on top of his cast while he grabs a spoon from the drawer and a bag of chips out of the cupboard. He checks the colt cam he rigged up before he leaves the room. Claire and Ziggy—they'd named the colt for the zigzag blaze running down his nose—are just standing together, everything right.

Quag heads upstairs. He stops and watches the moon floating outside the window. He climbs onto the bed and pulls out his phone.

He reads all of Cassie's texts again. He runs his finger over each blue oval. For a long time he looks at the last impossible text shouting "TALK TO ME QUAG" at him from the screen.

And then he calls Cassie.

And he talks to her.

THIRTY-EIGHT

A week ago, Quag sent off the eleven audio files on the phones to Cassie and the drama kids.

Now Quag sees that a file called EPIC AWESOMENESS has just come in on his phone from Mikey. It's a recording of a new radio play. Cassie and Mikey and Jax and Rhia have used every sound Quag sent. The way they used the crane chatter is way funny. It busts Quag up every single time he listens to it.

THIRTY-NINE

There are so many beautiful things in the world—solid women in Iowa diners flipping pancakes on a black griddle, sandhill cranes rising out of the mist, a sunset seen from a roof, the world spread out beneath a gyroplane, the sighing of wind in long grass—that you might not know until it happens that the most beautiful thing in the world is seeing someone you love, someone you thought you'd never see again, walk toward you down a Nebraska lane.

But that is what Quag is seeing right now—Cassie Byzinski, along with her Aunt Becca, getting out of a dusty red car and walking toward him.

Her sneakers poof through the dust, and Quag knows he should say something, but he is too busy smiling to quite manage that.

Cassie stops in front of him.

"Is your mom going to be okay?" she asks, her eyes, her face, as intense as ever.

"I think so," says Quag. "Maybe. Uncle Jay's helping."

Cassie looks around the yard, at the house, at the barn, taking everything in. But Quag is still standing on the porch steps, looking only at her, smiling like a doofus.

"Are you going to show me the creek?" she asks.

So he shows her the creek.

They walk down past the barn, and Quag takes Cassie to see Ziggy. Cassie sighs and puts her face right up against the little colt's curly face and then laughs when he snorts in her hair. And then he goes leaping and snorting all over the corral, just kicking his heels up, and Quag thinks, *That's exactly how I feel.* But you can only get away with that kind of stuff if you're a horse.

They walk down through the sweet grass, listening to it whisper secrets. They sit shoulder to shoulder on the bank of the creek for a long time just hearing the songs of the grass and the water braid together. And when Cassie leans her head against his shoulder, Quag feels the planets spin around them. Just up there spinning and spinning.

Later, as Quag stands and watches the car that holds Cassie disappear back into the east, Uncle Jay shuffles over in his boots and stands next to Quag. "There are not too many times in a man's life when a car carrying two people like *that* comes down the driveway," he says.

And Quag thinks that's probably true, so he watches that car until he can't even see the dust of it anymore.

BIRDS: JOURNEYS

Cranes aren't supposed to be alone. If you see one alone, it means something went wrong. Maybe the crane they were traveling with got sick or hurt, and they had to stay with them instead of lifting off with the rest of the flock. So then they ended up in the summer in a place they weren't supposed to be.

That's what Uncle Jay says probably happened to the crane down by the creek. But he also says the flocks come back through every year, and the birds that got left behind get picked back up by the group.

Anyway, that's how it works with cranes.

Quag used to think that birds just hung out. Like, here's my tree, and this is where I stay. Okay, he'd heard about migration, but he thought it was more like birds just spent a couple of months in Florida in the winter like some people's grandparents do.

But that's not how it is at all. There are whole pathways across the sky. Mind-bending journeys he knew nothing about. Blackpoll warblers weigh less than three sheets of paper, and they fly themselves across the Atlantic Ocean on their way to South America. Bar-tailed godwits fly from Alaska to New Zealand and don't stop once in the nine days it takes them. Arctic terns fly pole to pole every single year, so by the time they die, it's like they flew to the moon and back three times. Short-tailed shearwaters travel more than 18,000 miles in a year—but sometimes come back to the same burrow to nest. You can do that kind of thing when you have wings.

Nobody tells you about this stuff. Nobody sits you down when you're four and says, "Let me tell you about short-tailed shearwaters." But they should. Then you would know that the world is big and wild, and there are places you might go that you can't imagine yet.

Next spring, more than half a million sandhill cranes will fly through Nebraska on their way to Canada or Alaska or Siberia. Uncle Jay says there will be so many that some days it will look like someone is pouring them out of the sky, and you can't stop watching. Aunt Becca has always wanted to see that, has always wanted to photograph those cranes. It would supercharge that life list of hers. She had said so on that day when she and Cassie were here, and they'd all been sitting on the porch together before they'd left,

watching thunderheads roll across the long horizon. So Quag and Cassie have a plan. Because Quag is good at plans. They are going to make sure that happens.

They've got months to work on this together.

Couldn't be better.

A NOTE FROM THE AUTHOR

In my years of working with kids, I have met many young people like Quag—kids who were trying to hold up a whole lot of their world. And many of them, like Quag, had the idea that they shouldn't talk about what was going on, that they needed to work hard to keep it hidden. That's not true. Quag's mom has an undiagnosed bipolar disorder, and the fact that both she and Quag try to hide that keeps her (and Quag) from getting help for a long time.

So, here's the thing. There are going to be times in your life when you need some help—for any number of reasons. One of those reasons may be mental illness. One in five people have some type of mental illness. It's a pretty common thing, really. So, you may need help for yourself. Or you may need help for a friend or family member.

And there are people who will help. But sometimes you have to find them. If you have a trustworthy, kind, and practical adult in your life, start there. If you don't, you may want to begin by talking to a school counselor. Or you can call or text 988 for a confidential talk or chat with a crisis counselor. They also have a website: 988lifeline.org. Another great place to get information and help is NAMI.org. Check out their Teen and Young Adult Resource Directory and helpline while you're there. The Teen and Young Adult HelpLine can connect you with a young person with similar life experiences who can fill you in on resources and offer support.

If a friend is in a place where they don't realize they need help, but you realize that they do, you can offer to walk with them to the school counselor or help them talk to their parents or another adult. For immediate help in a crisis, call or text 988. Another way to help is to be there for them. Don't avoid them or be afraid to talk about what's going on. Talking matters. Talking helps. We'd all do better if we talked about mental health more. We talk about physical illnesses—diabetes, a broken arm, appendicitis—often with an openness that allows us to come together and help each other. Anyone can break an arm or leg. Anyone can have a mental illness. And the same kind of openness and support that helps us during a physical illness can help us with a mental illness.

The *way* we talk about it matters too. In this story, I chose to use some words that aren't the best, because I know that kids like Quag hear those words a lot. Words like "sicko" and "crazy." And those words hurt. Quag is hurt when Mikey uses the word "sicko," even though Mikey doesn't know about Quag's mom and isn't actually trying to hurt him. And Quag *is* trying to hurt his mom when he gets angry with her and calls her crazy. Maybe the best way to choose the words we use is to just assume that someone in any room we're in is affected by mental health issues: Because one in five, remember? It may seem like a small thing, but dropping words like "crazy" (and a whole bunch of other unkind terms we often use) from our vocabulary actually makes the world a little easier for all of us.

Wishing you all the best,
Mylisa

ACKNOWLEDGMENTS

So many, many people helped me with this book. Well-deserved shout-outs to the following people:

To Anne Hoppe, for being tough enough to insist on a good book and smart enough to help me make one. It is always a joy to work with you. Thank you.

To Erin Murphy, for introducing me to Anne and for being patient with what passes for "my process."

To the team at Clarion. To Mary Wilcox for her advocacy for this kid named Quagmire Tiarello. To cover artist Chris Choi for capturing Quag's side-eye, and to Chris Kwon and Jessie Gang for inspired design work (extra thanks for the birds, Chris!). To Erin DeWitt, Amy Reeve, Heather Tamarkin, and Mary Magrisso for help in catching errors and keeping me on schedule. And to the Marketing, Publicity, and Sales teams for putting the book in your hands, with special gratitude to Jennifer Sheridan.

A huge thank-you to Kelly Cook and Crystal Perrine, who helped me understand the realities of living with a loved one with bipolar disorder.

To Lauren Giannetti and Nicole Wise, who took the time to talk to me about the work they do on the front lines of the mental health care system and why they do it. I am so grateful.

To the brain trust who read a first draft and helped speed up my thinking about this book with their careful reading and questions: Sondra Soderborg, Christine Carron, Charlie Perryess.

To the Save the Quag team—Sondra Soderborg, Sharon Dembro, Louisa Jaggar, Charlie Perryess—who were gracious about lending both time and smarts during a well-now-I-am-*really*-stuck period during revisions.

To Lisze Bechtold and Louisa Jaggar, who kept me supplied with clocks that tell the day of the week, ginger chews, and laughter during a particularly sloggy part of the rewrite.

To Jackie Friedman Mighdoll, who sat with me on the question of structure. Thank you for taking the time to think aloud with me on the phone during a very busy and stressful week in your own life. And thank you for continuing to think after we got off the phone, so that the next morning you could text me the perfect idea.

To Tim Larsen, who gave me the game the drama kids play and who is the kind of person who would reengineer a Magic 8 Ball.

To Tim Manring, who answered a whole lot of questions about foaling. Best wishes to this year's new foals.

To Hyrum Jones, for introducing me to the wonder of gyroplanes.

To Stacy Schleusener, who answered questions about growing up in a small town in Nebraska and helped me see all the beautiful things that Quag is going to love about it.

To Patti Gauch, my teacher, who always believed that Quag was real.

And to Dave, for being there through all of it, and cooking dinner, and bringing me chocolate bars, and always believing it could be done.